FASHIONABLY LATE
A VICTORIAN CHRISTMAS ROMANCE

M. DIANE HARRIS

ROGUE WOLF

PUBLISHING

FASHIONABLY LATE

CONTENTS

Acknowledgments   ix

1. The Invitation   1
2. An Intriguing Stranger   11
3. Returning to Bentley Manor   17
4. An Eventful Sleigh Ride   23
5. Tete-a-Tete   35
6. Looming Clouds Overhead   43
7. Festivities Interrupted   49
8. A Night of Peril   55
9. A Race Against Nature   61
10. Embracing Calm After the Storm   67
11. Grandmother Bentley's Cozy Corner   75
12. A Delightful Dilemma   81
13. The Glasshouse   89
14. The Blue Danube Waltz   103
15. Inadvertent Enlightenment   113
16. Hudson's Pond   119
17. Setting Aside Protocol   131
18. Things Sorted Out   143
19. An Almost Perfect Christmas   149
20. The Twelve Days of Christmas   157
21. A New Year's Surprise   163
22. An Unforeseen Calamity   173
23. Navigating Through Difficult Waters   183
24. Jubilation or Lamentation   191
25. Journey to the Church   199
26. Epilogue—Three years later   207

Dedicated with love to Joe, my dear husband, and our amazing children
—Joey, John, Laura, Janel, and Carol

ACKNOWLEDGMENTS

Thank you to all who have encouraged and helped me in any way along the journey of creating this novel. Family names have been used throughout the story as a tribute to each of you, an expression of my love for my family. Some of the incidents I have written about have actually occurred, but I have placed them into the 1890 time period. All Rights reserved. Copyright 2024

THE INVITATION

*T*he world howled around Eliza Wentworth. Wrapped in a blanket with warm bricks at her feet, gusts of wind roared against her family's horse-drawn carriage. Even for December 1890, Amersham was dreadfully cold.

Eliza's teeth chattered, and despite her corset, bustle, bonnet, and wool coat, she was chilled to the bone. Tucking her hands deeper into her fur muff brought little relief. It made her wonder if going to town today was the right choice. However, once Eliza set her mind on something, she rarely wavered—a trait that had proven troublesome in the past.

She recalled her father purchasing a spirited horse when she was thirteen, and how she'd insisted on taming it. The day had ended with a lacerated chin, a bruised arm, and a near concussion after being thrown off the saddle nearly half-a-dozen times.

Her father had warned her, "One day your tenacity will get you into trouble."

And today, her tenacity had led to yet another unwise decision—all for the sake of fashion. Yet, who could blame her? She *needed* a suitable gown for the Season. She couldn't possibly appear at any Christmas parties wearing last year's style. It would be too gauche!

Eliza rested her forehead against the chilled glass of the carriage window, peering out at the desolate countryside.

Oh, how she yearned to visit Aunt Elizabeth in London and procure some exquisite evening gowns there. Her aunt, she was certain, would accompany her to all the finest shops.

In London, elegance reigned supreme. Amidst refined society, Eliza had found a white satin and lace creation with a graceful, cascading skirt that perfectly complimented her frame. It would be perfect for New Year's Eve.

But alas, in Amersham, she was limited to the modest establishments in town. At least visiting the local fabric shop was better than sitting around at home and enduring her parents' pestering about her unmarried state. By the way her mother fretted after her, one would think a life of spinsterhood was imminent.

The carriage came to a halt, and its door swung open. A gloved hand extended to Eliza. "Here you are." The young coachman attempted a smile, though his teeth chattered just as much as hers.

"Thank you, James," Eliza said, steadying herself as she stepped out. "I'm sorry for dragging you out here in this weather."

"N-not a problem, Miss Eliza." He shivered. "Glad to be of service." He gave her an approving nod. "When shall I expect your return?"

"I'll only be an hour!" Eliza called over her shoulder, rushing toward the fabric shop.

"But last time you took three!" the coachman shouted after her.

"An hour and a half, then!"

The coachman appeared unconvinced, but Eliza was already on her way, a bag of coins jingling in her pocket. She tried her best to avoid slipping on the icy cobblestones. A few laborers hurried by carrying sacks of grain and wheat. From the look of it, there weren't many people of Eliza's social standing out in Amersham's shopping district today.

The cold tended to keep the affluent away. One laborer side-stepped her, hurrying to load a barrel onto a horse-drawn buggy. "'Scuse me, miss." He then glanced up again and flashed a flirtatious smile.

Such encounters were not uncommon. Eliza often attracted the attention of men in Amersham, be they low-class workers or noblemen. She paid them no mind. After all, she'd been told since her childhood that she resembled her mother.

Her beautiful chestnut-colored hair, soft curls and reddish highlights, perfectly contrasted with her smooth ivory skin. Her perky upturned nose and heart-shaped lips gave her a slightly coquettish appearance, and her smile revealed a dimple. But it was her azure blue eyes framed by delicate lashes that captivated others with their sparkling warmth, reflecting her overall cheerful disposition. She was always immaculately dressed in the latest fashion and her trim figure garnered her more than her share of admiring looks.

Eliza quickened her steps along the street, stealing a glance at the apothecary shop as she passed. The jars in the window showcased vibrant bursts of color—ingredients for medicines that reminded Eliza of the striking fabrics she'd seen in London years ago.

For a moment, she considered checking if the chemist, Mr. Woolf, was in. However, she restrained herself. She didn't want to keep the coachman waiting. Whenever she and Mr. Woolf talked about medicine, time flew by, and half a day would pass in no time.

So she continued on.

Pushing open the doors of her favorite dress shop, she found relief from the cold. Mrs. Shaw's Dress Shop was virtually empty. Her fingers began to warm up as she thumbed through several bolts of fabric, searching for the perfect one. Hidden between two bolts of fabric, she spotted a rich cranberry silk with ruby undertones. It gleamed beneath the shop lights, reminding her of a gown she had seen in London.

"Miss Wentworth, it's a delight to see you, especially on such a cold winter day," Mrs. Shaw, the proprietor, welcomed her as she approached. A measuring tape was draped casually around her high-neck, deep-purple dress, accented by intricate lace trim. At the top of the lace was a simple broach. Her slightly graying hair sat high on her head in a bun.

"How are your parents? Are they surviving this cold weather?"

Mrs. Shaw asked as she neatly refolded a bolt of fabric to be put back on the shelf.

"They're well, but worried about me as usual. I keep reminding them that I'm perfectly able to find my own companions, but they continue inviting unattached young men to dinner. They encourage me to attend balls and parties, but I much prefer those in London."

"Oh, and why is that?" Mrs. Shaw peered over the glasses perched on her nose.

"Because there is a greater number and diversity of people."

"Well, perhaps this holiday season will prove to be more to your liking," Mrs. Shaw remarked, looking at the silk fabric Eliza had placed on the cutting table.

"I suppose," she answered without much conviction. "My family has certain traditions we do each year. It would be nice to do something different for a change. The bright spot is that my sister and her husband are coming for Christmas. I'm anxious to see their new baby. There is something about having a baby around that is so delightful."

"Jolly good, Miss Wentworth," she said as she unrolled a new bolt of luxurious cranberry velvet fabric. "This just arrived from London. Why don't you stand over by the mirror and see how you would look in it?"

"I do like it," she said, viewing herself from various angles in the nearby mirror. "But I prefer the cranberry silk."

"Very good. It will make a lovely gown. Shall I bill it to your family's account, as always?" Mrs. Shaw asked, while measuring and cutting the fabric.

"Yes, please do."

Taking the package wrapped in brown paper and tied with twine, Eliza thanked Mrs. Shaw, wishing her a Happy Christmas. After leaving the shop, Eliza saw James waiting with the carriage.

"Up you go," he said, clearly enjoying his job of transporting her about.

As the coach bumped along, Eliza could see little patches of snow dotting the ground, and the distant hills looking hazy under a gray sky. She tried ignoring the chill in the air, but it was no good.

"Thank goodness," she murmured, seeing Wentworth Manor ahead.

Even on this dismal day, her home was a splendid example of a Queen Anne design with its asymmetrical face of red brick. As the coach passed by the majestic trees acting as sentinels, their branches now bare, she felt relief seeing the welcoming porch.

She thought of how dearly she loved her home, especially the many adventures she had as a child. She would pretend it was a castle. Her imaginary play often got her in trouble. Climbing the trellis of ivy adorning the walls, she crushed some of her mother's precious purple pansies. There were times she was scolded for becoming a nuisance in the kitchen as she went searching for treats in the storage tins, which were a necessity for the afternoon tea parties with her dolls. Her dolls often suffered from imaginary wounds, which, along with their tea, needed patching up. Pretending to be their nurse, Eliza would care for them by using scraps of fabric for bandages.

Eliza quickly made her way from the coach to the manor's main entrance. As she entered through the doorway, the warmth of the house welcomed her like a gentle embrace by the sun.

"Eliza, you look chilled to the bone," her mother observed, looking up from her stitchery. "What a day to venture out. Here, come sit by the hearth and I'll ring for tea." Mrs. Wentworth patted a deep green chair, took off the chenille throw, and wrapped it around Eliza's shoulders. Dressed in her usual, simple muslin shirtwaist day-dress, with a cameo pinned at her neck, Mrs. Wentworth's attire reflected her practical nature. Only on occasions like receiving guests, going on visits, or attending church did Mrs. Wentworth dress more formally. Her lovely chestnut-colored hair was pulled back in waves, secured by two tortoise shell combs. Despite her unpretentious appearance, her beauty shone through, with her engaging smile and warm hazel eyes that endeared her to others.

"It looks like you've found the fabric you wanted," she commented, handing Eliza a dainty Dresden cup filled with her favorite Ceylon tea.

After taking a few sips of tea, Eliza hurriedly undid the twine.

"What's this?" she said, holding up a box of chocolates with a note attached. "It's from Mrs. Shaw, thanking us for our business."

"I am sure she only does this for her best customers," Mrs. Wentworth said, exhibiting a rare display of pride.

Eliza set the chocolates on a nearby end table and handed her mother the fabric. "Mrs. Shaw likes to help me with my selections, but I managed quite well on my own," she remarked confidently.

"It's lovely, dear, but did you really need another gown? I've lost count of the number you have. Surely there are more essential things to buy. I remember when you were younger, you ran about the manor or rode horses rather recklessly. Your clothes were in constant need of repair. Now you've become an elegant young woman whose expertise is fashion."

"Really, Mother, I have channeled my unrefined spirit into ladylike behavior, and you are still unsatisfied," Eliza sighed. "Father never says anything about what I purchase, and we never seem to lack money."

"True, true, but I do wish your father would be a little more practical, just the same." Mrs. Wentworth rarely commented on her husband's extravagant tastes in wanting the newest and the finest.

"Oh, I almost forgot. While you were in town, this came for you." Mrs. Wentworth handed Eliza a linen envelope with *Miss Wentworth* written in elegant calligraphy. It was sealed with rich brown wax, sparkling with bits of gold and stamped with the initial *B*.

"I wonder who it's from? The only family I can think of are the Boutons and they are away for the month," Eliza mused.

"Well, there is only one way to find out, Eliza. You've been wanting something special to look forward to this holiday season, and now it has presented itself," her mother said.

Breaking the seal and opening the envelope she silently read the invitation. "Mother, it's from Lord Thomas Bentley. Oh my goodness, it's been nearly three years since we last corresponded! He's invited me to a Christmas celebration at Bentley Manor from the fourteenth to the eighteenth of December. He writes that there will be outdoor activities, a musical soiree as well as a Christmas ball, and he is looking forward to renewing our acquaintance."

"It's curious we didn't know about his return. I'm usually aware of such comings and goings," her mother said.

The invitation brought back memories of a similar one Eliza had opened when she was seventeen, inviting her to her first debutante ball being held in London. She and her closest friend, Julia, were excited about their First Season among the ton.

While attending the ball, Eliza met Thomas Bentley and his cousin, Emmett Bentley. The Bentley name came with a well-established reputation and carried with it considerable influence. She had heard of a Bentley Estate near Amersham, which had been maintained but not occupied for several years.

Emmett Bentley was a polished, attractive man with a flair for flamboyance. His infectious energy and charming ways caught the attention of many debutantes, yet he managed to elude any romantic entanglements. Eliza enjoyed his company, but had no amorous thoughts towards him.

Thomas Bentley, on the other hand, possessed an air of self-assuredness. His striking good looks, dark hair, and piercing brown eyes made him seem unapproachable, almost stuffy. His reserved manner was unnerving.

Despite his being four years her senior, Julia was infatuated with Thomas. Eliza was astounded at their growing attachment and tried to discourage Julia. "What do you even talk about? Business in London or the weather?"

Julia only laughed. "Don't be silly. Mr. Bentley is easy to talk to. He possesses warmth and kindness, and is so interesting. He knows so much about many things, and we rarely lack for conversation." Eventually, Eliza became satisfied with the happiness that her friend had found and trusted in her good judgment. At the conclusion of the London Season, Julia and Thomas became engaged.

The following spring, an elaborate wedding was held in London for the much-touted couple. Being Maid of Honor, Eliza met many esteemed guests, including Lord Harold Bentley and Lady Bentley,

Thomas's grandparents. She found out they owned the Bentley Estate in Amersham, but were moving to Hastings to enjoy a milder climate and sea air. This was necessary because of Lord Bentley's declining health, due to a respiratory illness.

Returning for a Second Season in London was not pleasant for Eliza. She no longer had her good friend to share her thoughts with or give each other advice. She visited Julia and Thomas and was often a guest in their home, but of course, things were not the same.

Eliza wanted to find the same happiness Julia was experiencing as a young wife, and wanted more than endless balls and parties. She wanted to form an attachment without making it a matter of convenience, but with someone she really loved. To her delight, a young man caught her attention, and they sought each other's company. Their future looked promising, until it became public that his family was embroiled in financial troubles. As a result, Mr. Wentworth insisted she return home and distance herself from the situation. Determined not to repeat the disillusionment of her Second Season, she did not return to London for a Third Season.

Her trips to London became more seldom when Thomas, upon his grandfather's passing, inherited the Bentley's estate in Amersham, as well as his title. Because Julia and Thomas resided there, Eliza was able to visit them often, and she rejoiced when their two children, Edward and Pamela, were born.

Then Julia's health began declining due to issues associated with childbirth. Tragically, she passed away ten months after Pamela was born. Devastated, Lord Bentley immediately took his children and went to London to live with his parents. Eliza had not only lost her best friend, but had lost contact with the Bentley family, as well.

She reread the invitation, bringing her back to the present. "I am surprised to be invited. I want to attend, but I won't feel comfortable." As she often did when excessively happy or nervous, Eliza fidgeted with the invitation.

"It seems only natural that you would be invited, considering you were Julia's best friend and treated the children like an aunt would. How old are they now?" her mother asked.

"Edward is six and Pamela is four. I can't go. It would just be too hard without Julia's presence. To be sociable with Lord Bentley after a three-year absence is also something I don't want to deal with. I'll write a note of regret," she said.

"That would be a breach of etiquette, Eliza. After all, Lord Thomas Bentley is trying to reestablish himself again in the neighborhood. You really must go. You most certainly could be a help to them, and I'm sure you will find it satisfying to reconnect with the family."

After some moments of contemplation, Eliza admitted, "You're right, Mother. I will go." Then she brightened up. "Besides, now I have somewhere to wear my new gown."

"We need to get the fabric to Christine immediately," Mrs. Wentworth said. "She's so busy this time of year. I hear that her dressmaking services are really in demand now that she has a new treadle sewing machine and can take on more clients."

Clutching the precious fabric, Eliza climbed the staircase to her bedchamber. Her mind was churning with questions. As a widower, what would Lord Bentley be like? Surely, living in London, he'd had opportunities to marry again. With his title and good looks, there would be many women attracted to such a man. And what of the children? Would Edward even remember her?

These questions could only be answered when she was once again at Bentley Manor.

AN INTRIGUING STRANGER

*E*liza dropped the fabric off at Christine's shop the next day she was in town. Having another excuse to go shopping, she brimmed with excitement to find fun and memorable activities to do with the Bentley children. Soon her basket was full of supplies for making Christmas cards, paper cones, two porcelain dolls, and tin soldiers.

She balanced the many bags of treats and trinkets in her arms as she crossed the cobblestone street, the cold biting at her face. The clopping hooves and neighing of horses subsided as Eliza reached the last stretch of shops.

Stopping under a lamp post, she rubbed her cheeks, attempting to get some feeling back in her face. She saw icicles on the post next to her. They reminded her of when she and Julia were girls and used to dare each other to stick their tongues on icicles. One time, Eliza had stood outside for over an hour because her tongue had gotten stuck. The memory made Eliza smile, but it also brought aching in her heart.

She had already picked over nearly every boutique and toy shop in town and was now scanning the last few stores on Market Street for any place she may have missed. Coming toward her was a wagon jostling along on the cobblestones, filled to the brim with wooden furniture. As the wagon passed by, Eliza noticed a man in a navy cap steering the horses forward, weaving them around patches of ice on the street. He was broad-shouldered with an imposing frame. It reminded her of someone she knew.

As Eliza traveled home, the fleeting image of the man she thought she recognized lingered in her mind. She couldn't quite place him, and was distracted by the puzzle of his identity. Determined to focus on the tasks ahead, including her plans for the coming week, she pushed the mystery aside.

A few days later, she returned to town and remembered the intriguing stranger. She began puzzling over his identity once more, but still couldn't place him. Eliza stopped by the vicarage to donate hand-made knitted hats and scarves as well as a pouch of money. Knitting was one of the homemaking skills in which she had found success.

"Thank you ever so much for your generosity, Miss Wentworth. It is very kind of you," Vicar Pike said. Her donation was modest compared to the recent substantial contributions made by her father and others who donated toward the addition of new pews, but Eliza was determined to do her own small part.

As her coach pulled away from the vicarage, she spied a man wearing a tweed jacket and navy cap working hard as he loaded a wagon in the adjoining courtyard. He was facing away from her and she couldn't see his face closely. She wondered why the mystery man seemed so familiar. Perhaps it was because he resembled the man she had seen a few days prior.

"Oh, well, it can't be anyone I know. No one of my acquaintances would engage in such a menial task," she sighed and continued on her way.

The next two weeks passed quickly. Eliza's anticipation of going to Bentley Manor began to bubble over like a pot of porridge on the stove. With Daisy, her lady's maid's help, she had selected and reselected her wardrobe. Daisy's youth and efficient manner were compatible with Eliza and they had become friends. Her curly red hair and Irish brogue made her heritage evident. Her grandparents had immigrated to England during the Great Potato Famine in 1850.

"Daisy, we need to do something different for a bit," Eliza announced, heading to the parlor, where a large fir tree stood in one corner of the room, begging to be decorated.

"Och, it's a grand tree, that is! A fine one for decorating." Despite its elegance, the parlor was warm and inviting. Blue baroque wallpaper accented with a geometric gold pattern was offset by velvet drapes with valances trimmed with gold tassels. Two housemaids had hung a few ornaments, but were called away on other duties.

"Daisy, would you lend me a hand with these?" Eliza asked, handing her a box of German handmade ornaments.

"What be they made from?" Daisy's eyes fixed on one shaped like an apple.

"They are hand-blown glass ornaments made in Germany called Kugels. On my last trip to London, I found them. It's said that Queen Victoria has similar ornaments on the Royal Christmas tree in memory of Prince Albert." She attached ones shaped like tear drops, pine cones, bells, and birds.

Daisy held up a small glass ornament with a ribbon tied at the top. "What about this bauble shaped like a pickle?"

"That's another German tradition, and a fun one. The pickle is hidden among the branches for the children to find. The first to do so receives a special gift."

"But we've got no children here." Daisy stated the obvious.

"Then we adults will have to do it for now."

Eliza thought about Daisy's words that there were no children there. That was something she was beginning to long for. While living with her parents was secure and pleasant, she was getting restless for a change. By now, she should be the mistress of her own home. Margaret, just two years younger, had married Lord Ainsley and had a baby. Perhaps, she should have returned to London for the Third Season, but then she thought how useless it was to dwell on past decisions.

Something was pawing on the edge of her skirt. "Oh, it's you,

Winston," she said, kneeling and hugging their beloved dog. She was always amused at his regal velvet collar with gold embroidery. Her father thought it only proper for his thoroughbred English Cocker Spaniel.

While glitter paper angels and stars, pinecones and garland were placed on the tree, Winston busied himself with a strand of tinsel. Before long, he was tangled up, looking like a poorly-wrapped present.

"Eliza, you've outdone yourself. The tree looks magnificent." Mr. Wentworth strolled into the room and rescued Winston from his self-inflicted predicament.

She looked up at her father, appreciating how well he kept his appearance. His light brown hair was carefully combed in such a way that flattered his face. His high cheekbones and strong jawline were impressive. Even at home, he wore expertly cut waistcoats of the finest fabrics, along with carefully tied cravats. Along with looking younger than his age, he had the talent for putting anyone at ease.

"I understand you were in town today, Eliza," he said, easing into his favorite well-worn over-stuffed chair, a contented Winston sitting at his feet.

"Yes, I bought supplies to make Christmas cards with Edward and Pamela when I'm at the Christmas Celebration."

"Did you note how much you spent?" Mr. Wentworth asked.

"No," Eliza looked surprised. "I just had the clerks put it on the ledger like I always do. I did the same with the fabric I purchased from Mrs. Shaw's Dress Shop earlier this month. Isn't that what you've asked me to do?" She was taken aback by her father's inquiry.

"Yes, of course, dear. I was just curious." Her father quickly changed the subject. "Is that current cake I smell?" Winston's head popped up when he heard the word 'cake.'

"Yes, it's freshly baked," Mrs. Wentworth announced, as a kitchen maid brought in a tray of cake and tea. Seeing Winston's biscuit on a fancy plate, she said, exasperated, "Honestly, sometimes I feel like the dog gets more attention than we do."

"Well, dear, he is a favorite of the staff." Mr. Wentworth laughed.

"And we are not?" his wife countered, putting her hands on her hips.

"Of course we are, dear. You're especially loved by myself and everyone else here."

She rewarded her husband with a kiss on the cheek.

Contentment filled the room as the three of them enjoyed each other's company, listening to Winston gnawing on his biscuit. As the evening settled in and the gas lights were lit, Eliza felt a profound sense of gratitude for time spent with her parents, and how fortunate she was to be their daughter. Heading to her bedchamber to prepare for the night, she reflected on how stable, almost predictable, her life had been for quite some time and entertained the thought that perhaps the coming year would bring new opportunities.

Eliza's thoughts then turned to the man she saw earlier in town, driving the wagon of furniture. Though she had only seen the back of his head, she couldn't shake the feeling that she had encountered him somewhere before.

She dismissed the matter as an unsettling feeling began to take hold. Eliza wondered what it would be like to see Lord Bentley again. She hoped for the reunion to be a positive one. With that in mind, she began debating which dresses to take—the lavender day dress, the beige linen dress, or both? She also considered her navy skirt and white top, three dinner dresses, and a traveling suit. Would her evening gown be ready in time? Would she need several coats, and where had she put her wellies? Her mind swirled in a whirlpool of thoughts and emotions. Eventually, she fell asleep, her dreams whisking her to the ball in her new gown, only to realize she was barefoot. What a nightmare!

RETURNING TO BENTLEY MANOR

*E*liza rested her head on the velvet cushion perched atop the coach seat, observing Daisy's attempt to be comfortable as they traveled. The coach jostled over the uneven road, bouncing up and down, causing Eliza to grasp a nearby leather strap for support. This rough road lasted only a few minutes. As she gazed out at the snow-clad landscape, she noticed scattered homes dotting the scenery.

The closer they drew to the Bentley Manor, Eliza's unease grew. She fidgeted with the edge of her scarf, anxiously glancing out the window.

"Daisy, is my hair still in place? I'm worried the bouncing of the coach has made a mess of it."

"Ah, dinnae worry, Miss Eliza, it's as neat as ever," Daisy replied with an assuring smile. "You look just right."

Eliza sighed. "Do you think Lord Bentley will greet us tonight or wait until the morning? It is getting quite late."

"I'd say he'll come tonight. I wouldn't fret too much."

"I've been thinking how to greet him," Eliza admitted and then continued with a determined nod of her head. "I think the wisest thing to do is let him lead the way."

Daisy nodded her head in agreement, removing some food from a small woven basket.

"Miss Eliza, why don't ye have some of the food that was packed for us? T'will do ya good." She handed Eliza a tray with cheese and apples on it.

After taking a few nibbles, Eliza set her tray down. Viewing the red-orange sunset, which added color to the winter sky, Eliza began to feel a sense of peace. Her thoughts shifted from seeing Lord Bentley without Julia's presence to the pleasure of seeing Edward and Pamela again. She gradually drifted into a light doze.

"We've arrived, we have!" Daisy exclaimed, waking Eliza with a start.

Peering out of the coach window, she was astonished to see the manor glowing like a lighthouse in a storm. The gas sconces and lanterns radiated a warm inviting light against the backdrop of the inky-black sky.

"I can do this," she muttered, adjusting her hat. Soon, she and Daisy were passing through the massive entryway doors, decorated with two large wreaths that were trimmed with pine cones and slices of dried oranges and apples.

They entered the foyer with its intricate wood paneling stretching before them. The chandeliers overhead cast reflections on the polished marble floors. At the center stood an antique table, graced with a lovely fresh flower arrangement. Just beyond that was a grand staircase splitting into two separate flights with a landing in-between.

"Welcome to Bentley Manor, Miss Wentworth, Miss Maloney. It is a pleasure to have you here." Kingsley, the tall, dignified butler with slightly graying hair greeted them. He had been a part of the Bentley household for as long as Eliza could remember.

To her way of thinking, he was the perfect butler, always anticipating the family's needs. On one of her previous visits, the weather had been mild and she had not brought along a shawl. When it was time to leave, the air was much cooler, and Kinsley had put a blanket in her coach. When she unfolded it, three small bars of chocolate fell out. Ever since then, he had endeared himself to her.

"Hello, Kingsley. I am glad to be back. I see everything is in perfect order."

"The staff has been busy preparing for this event. I will tell Lord Bentley of your arrival," Kingsley said before disappearing down the marble hallway. Eliza watched her trunk being carried into the manor, realizing she had brought an excessive amount of clothing for such a short stay.

The familiar scent of polished wood and old tapestries enveloped Eliza as she stood in the entryway of Bentley Manor. Every intricate inlay design in the wood panels brought back memories, and the absence of Julia momentarily overwhelmed her. Taking a deep breath to steady herself, and feeling the support of Daisy's presence, she felt calmer. The house was still, except for quiet, deliberate footsteps approaching her from the shadows.

Suddenly, she caught sight of Lord Bentley. When he reached her, he took her hand and bowed slightly. His eyes met hers, and the years apart, along with the reality of current circumstances, pierced her very soul.

"Miss Wentworth, I am glad you are here for the Christmas celebration, and welcome to you as well, Daisy." His tone was formal yet cordial, his deep, masculine voice, unmistakable.

"It's a pleasure being here, Lord Bentley. I was delighted to receive your invitation and to learn you had returned to Amersham." She felt a rush of mixed emotions—sadness, relief, and hope that the next few days would bridge the gap in their association.

"My parents send their greetings, and want to host your family for dinner very soon," she added, aiming to make things more comfortable for both of them.

"That would be a pleasure. I look forward to seeing your parents again," Thomas said.

As she gazed into his dark brown eyes, she recalled she only came to his chin, where he had a dimple. His dark brown, thick hair was expertly styled, adding to his striking appearance. His beige waistcoat fit perfectly, accentuating his broad shoulders. He was even more dashing than she had remembered. Julia had often remarked how fortunate she was to have such a handsome husband. All the little speeches Eliza had prepared fled her mind like baby sparrows from the nest.

"I have noticed many changes since my return. Fortunately, in my absence, my steward, Mr. Harrison, has overseen the manor," Thomas said. "Kingsley and Mrs. Adams have been invaluable, as well."

His self-assured demeanor was intimidating. She had known him long enough to be familiar with his constant propriety. As she listened, she began fidgeting with the glove she had just removed, twisting it gently in her hands. "Have your parents come for the holidays?"

"No. They're not fond of bumpy six-hour coach rides, especially in the winter. But my cousin Emmett and my brother Daniel, his wife, and daughter are here," Thomas replied with pleasure.

"How delightful. I haven't seen your cousin or brother's family for a number of years, and look forward to being reacquainted with them again."

"Daniel's family moved from London and now reside in Chesham, just three miles away. We have tried convincing my parents to move here as well, but they feel it is a little too provincial for them and prefer the city. They are Londoners through and through." Thomas shook his head.

"Change can be difficult. Other than occasional visits to London, I've lived in Amersham my entire life, and can't imagine living any other place," Eliza said with a thoughtful expression.

"At times, moves are necessary," Thomas acknowledged. She realized it was something he did not wish to talk about further.

"I am anxious to see Edward and Pamela again. They must bring you a great deal of joy," she said.

"They are a handful, but I am grateful for them. Edward goes by Ned now. It just seems to suit him better."

Then he looked past Eliza out the door as the luggage was being brought in. "It's getting late." Thomas frowned. "I'll call for Mrs. Adams."

Soon, the head housekeeper appeared, wearing a modest cap that neatly secured her hair, now sprinkled with gray. She moved a bit slower, but in no other way had changed. She was just as congenial as she had been in the past when Eliza visited the manor.

"If you will follow me, Miss Wentworth," Mrs. Adams said, "I'll show you to your bedchamber. A room on the third floor in the staff's quarters has been prepared for Daisy."

"Thank you, Mrs. Adams," Eliza replied as she and Daisy followed her up the staircase with its polished mahogany banister. The frosted glass gaslights nestled in ornate sconces lit the way. Eliza's familiarity with the manor guided her instinctively up the staircase. Her mind swirled as she recalled the many times she and Julia had climbed these stairs to go to the library. There they shared laughter, secrets, and lively discussions.

At the top of the landing, something caught Eliza's attention. Prominently displayed was a stunning portrait of Julia, a new addition since her last visit. Wrestling with her emotions, she struggled to hold back the tears that were close to spilling.

Turning from the portrait, Eliza walked along the hallway and recognized the familiar paintings of the English countryside adorning the walls, placed there during Julia's redecoration of the manor.

Simultaneously, Thomas had overseen the installation of practical updates such as iron-steam radiators and a plumbing system. Julia was certain the radiators would detract from the ambiance of the manor, but Thomas wisely chose ornately designed radiators that would blend in. The townsfolk buzzed with excitement as the estate modernized. Eliza looked forward to enjoying such luxuries as running hot water, not yet in her home.

As Eliza stepped into the bedchamber she exclaimed, "What a lovely room!" Running her hand along the post of the four-poster bed topped with a silky turquoise cover she added, "Blue is my favorite color. It's as if the room has been designed just for me." Two sapphire-blue armchairs, printed with delicate patterns, sat near a tea table. Most inviting was a lounge chaise placed by the cast-iron fireplace, which dated back to the late seventeen-hundreds when Thomas's great-grandfather had the manor built.

"Where are the Christmas decorations?" Eliza blurted out.

"I believe Lord Bentley has an outing planned to gather evergreens and decorate them," Mrs. Adams replied.

"Oh, I see," Eliza murmured meekly, embarrassed by her outspokenness. Mrs. Adams just smiled and instructed Daisy to continue following her.

Once her nightly routine was completed, Eliza pondered the conversation she'd had earlier with Lord Bentley. He seemed congenial enough. At least, the first contact had been successfully navigated. Could she deal with his impenetrable, reserved manner? He had expressed a desire to start a new life with his children.

Hoping to contribute, for her dear departed friend Julia, at least, Eliza considered offering to come read with Ned and Pamela. She had also made a list of excellent tutors, should they be needed. Her parents had expressed a desire to host the family for dinner during the holidays.

"I think those ideas should be quite satisfactory," she said aloud. Wrapping herself in a comforting quilt, Eliza created a cozy haven from the world outside.

AN EVENTFUL SLEIGH RIDE

elightful smells greeted Eliza as she entered the dining room. Sunlight streamed through the windows trimmed with swag drapes, a stunning contrast to the green, embossed wallpaper. On either side of Lord Bentley sat two lively children.

"Miss Wentworth, please come join us," Thomas said, standing. He seemed to be looking at her curiously and Eliza patted her hair, wondering if there was a strand or two out of place.

"Good morning. It appears I am late," she acknowledged with a tone of slight embarrassment.

"As there is no set time for breakfast, you are only fashionably late, Miss Wentworth." She gave Thomas a grateful look. He guided her to a sumptuous buffet of bacon, eggs, haddock, fruits, and breads. A tray of crumpets, hot from the skillet, appeared from the kitchen and was offered by a footman to each guest.

"May I help you be seated?" A man she recognized as Emmett Bentley stood and pulled out the chair next to him. His abundance of brown, curly hair hugging his neckline was just as she remembered it, but now he sported a small mustache. He had a Bentley look about him, but had a style all his own, dressed in a rust-colored jacket and carefully-tied cravat.

"Thank you, Mr. Bentley."

"It's a pleasure to see you again," he murmured quietly, pushing in her chair. "You look as lovely as ever." His comment brought back memories of London, boosting her confidence.

Thomas tapped on his glass. "I have the pleasure of introducing Miss Eliza Wentworth, a close family friend." Turning to his children he added, "Miss Wentworth and your mother grew up together."

"I used to come and visit your family. At times I would read stories to you," Eliza shared, hoping to invoke some kind of reaction.

Pamela sat quietly and Ned gave her a slight smile. She had been hoping for a bit more, perhaps some recognition from Ned. Pamela's delicate features, eyes as green as summer grass, and flaxen ringlets, reminded Eliza of Julia. With his dark hair and piercing brown eyes, Ned looked very much like his father. The reality of seeing them bereft of their mother immediately brought a wave of emotion that tugged at her heartstrings.

Thomas continued introducing her around the table. "You and my cousin have formerly met as well as my brother and his wife, Lily."

"Welcome, Miss Wentworth. It's good to see you again. Let me introduce you to our daughter, Abigail," Daniel said with a proud smile.

Next was Admiral Saunders, a retired naval officer and his lovely wife, Susan, and their daughter, Jane. Eliza was informed Miss Saunders was about to enter her first season in London.

Pamela climbed onto her father's knee and snuggled her face on his shoulder. Eliza observed that Thomas, usually so reserved and proper, now displayed unexpectedly open warmth and affection towards his daughter.

"I've brought some activities to do with you, children," Eliza said enthusiastically. "Perhaps we can even have a treasure hunt, with your father's permission, of course," she added with an impish grin.

"What's a treasure hunt?" Abigail asked.

"Some clues or little hints are hidden in several places in the house that guide you to the next place you need to look until you discover the treasure box," Eliza explained.

"What's in the box?" Ned asked, now adding his voice to the conversation.

"Little surprises like toys and treats. Ned, if your father has a magnifying glass, you can lead the hunt." He beamed at the prospect. Thomas had a thoughtful look and put his hand on his chin. "I'm sure with Kingsley's help I can locate one somewhere."

"I want to look for treasure, too," Abigail said with anticipation.

"You most certainly will be included, Abigail," Thomas assured her. Pamela wiggled off his lap.

Ned's enthusiasm was evident with his eager eyes, and his quick movement, jumping up from the table. "Can we go on a treasure hunt today, Papa?"

"We will, son, I promise, but today I have something else planned that you will enjoy as well. We're going on a sleigh ride to the woods to collect evergreens to decorate the manor."

"That should be done by the staff," Emmett said haughtily. "Certainly, we aren't expected to use saws and axes ourselves." He looked very offended.

Thomas, however, remained unruffled by his cousin's ungracious remarks. "True, the staff would usually handle that," Thomas replied, "but why shouldn't we enjoy being outdoors? They can help us when we return. Those who would care to join, please meet in front of the manor in thirty minutes, where two sleighs will be waiting."

Eliza and the others left the room. Though Eliza did notice, before Emmett left, he gave Thomas a very uncomfortable stare.

As she entered her bedchamber to exchange her puffed-sleeved blouse for a warm knit gray sweater and tweed midi-skirt, a flicker of movement outside the window caught her eye. Two sleighs, their runners glinting in the winter sunlight, moved from the stables nestled a short distance from the manor. Eliza thought, *What a delightful day this promises to be.*

After adjusting her cotton stockings and pulling on sturdy ankle-high boots, she wiggled her arms into her brown mid-length wool coat and picked up her brown leather gloves, hurrying off to join the others.

Outside, she felt a brisk breeze that made her catch her breath. Ahead were the sleighs with Thomas standing alongside one of them. Realizing she was the last to arrive, she smiled and said, "It looks like I'm fashionably late again. I hope I haven't kept you waiting."

"We're just now preparing to get underway." Scrutinizing her outfit he paused and said, "You look suitably dressed."

She wasn't quite sure how to react to such a comment. Was it a compliment, or was he just observing she had dressed warmly enough for their excursion?

Thomas invited her to ride in the sleigh along with Emmett and the children. While he loaded the children in, Emmett, having come out after all for the sleigh ride, was instantly by Eliza's side, helping her climb into the sleigh and settle onto the seat behind the driver, next to the children.

"That should keep you warm," he said, handing her a fur lap robe and smiling in a most charming way before taking a seat next to Thomas. Emmett looked quite satisfied, but Thomas did not.

"Papa, I want to sit next to you, " Ned said, climbing up beside his father.

Thomas settled his son between him and Emmett. "Ned, you can help me guide the horses."

"Here, Thomas." Daniel handed his brother a bow saw, an ax, and a tree pruner. "Do you need anything else before we get going?"

"Yes," Thomas muttered under his breath, "Please tell Emmett I'll attend to the comfort of my guests. His assistance is not necessary."

Daniel, trying to smooth things over so that Thomas would enjoy the day, said, "Well, maybe Emmett is just trying to be helpful."

"He could choose to be a little less helpful!" Thomas replied, as he urged the horses forward as Daniel shook his head, with a perplexed expression before climbing into the other sleigh.

Once underway, as the sleighs glided through the wintry countryside. Eliza turned to get Pamela's and Abigail's attention. "We'll have such fun today, collecting pine boughs. We might possibly see a squirrel, white hare, a duck, or even a woodpecker."

"A woodpecker! What's that?" Pamela asked. Evidently her life in London had not included identifying wildlife.

"It's a black bird with red and white feathers on top of its head, and pecks on trees to find food."

"Have you seen a woodpecker?" Pamela asked.

"Yes. But mostly I've heard one." Eliza said with a twinkle in her eye. "When I was about your age, one made its nest in a tree near my window. Every morning I woke up to its pecking. It was impossible to sleep with all that racket going on!"

"Did the woodpecker stay?" Pamela was now wide-eyed.

"For a while, but when it found a new home, it flew away. At last, I could sleep as long as I wanted. But you know what?"

"What?" Pamela and Abigail said in unison.

"I missed that silly woodpecker and kept listening for its pecking. It never did return."

Pamela and Abigail were excited, expecting to spot a woodpecker at any moment. They were delighted to see three mallard ducks playing in a small pond and gave each one a name. They waved goodbye to the ducks, the bracing wind whooshing in their faces as the horses trotted along.

As they chatted about woodpeckers and searched for animals, Eliza told the girls to call her by her Christian name. The formality of them addressing her as Miss Wentworth seemed as out of place as wearing a warm fur coat on a hot summer day.

The woods, dense with evergreen trees, dusted with a light sprinkling of snow, created a winter scene that looked like a master artist had painted it. Once the sleighs came to a stop, the children climbed out and began darting about to see who could find the best tree. While he hitched the horses to a sturdy tree, hanging a small bag of oats on the horses' harnesses, Thomas told his children to stay nearby where he could see them.

The area was soon busy with activity with cut branches scattered everywhere. Eliza found the tree she thought would be perfect as a Christmas tree. As she pulled a branch aside, she ended up with a handful of needles in her glove.

"This tree is dead." Thomas startled her as he walked up alongside her. "If you look closely, you will see the trunk is brown." As he brushed branches aside, more needles dropped off. Standing close to him, the chill in the air made their breaths intertwine. She felt a sudden attraction pulling her toward Thomas. Reigning her wandering thoughts that were drifting about like dandelion seeds when blown on, she focused back on the dead tree.

"When we were boys," Thomas said, looking over to where Pamela was playing beside Abigail, "Daniel and I cut down a similar evergreen tree and brought it home to decorate. Every time we attached an ornament, needles would drop off."

"I can't imagine your mother was very happy with pine needles all over the floor," she laughed.

"Not at all. We finally dragged the brittle thing out and chopped it into firewood. Next time, with the help of my father, we brought home a fresh evergreen tree that met my mother's approval." He glanced over to where Pamela had been playing, and his body went stiff. Eliza followed his gaze and saw Pamela was no longer there.

"Have you seen Pamela?" Thomas asked, hurrying over to Lily.

"She was here just a minute ago," Lily said, looking around.

"She can't have gone far," Daniel said, quickly instructing everyone to spread out and to go in different directions. "Be careful not to get lost—your footprints will guide you back. Lily, please stay here with Ned and Abigail, and ring the emergency bell in the sled when Pamela is found. Thomas, we'll find her," Daniel assured his brother.

Eliza was alarmed to see how quickly a child could disappear, and dashed off among the trees, knocking snow off them while branches cracked underfoot. The woods that looked so inviting on their arrival, now looked dense and menacing, muffling the sound of Eliza's voice. Pamela could be anywhere, and Eliza fought against the hopeless feeling of being overwhelmed. It didn't take long before her feet were becoming numb from the melting snow that crept into her boots.

"Pamela! Pamela!" she shouted until she was almost hoarse.

Stopping to catch her breath, she started again, determined with adrenaline to continue on. Looking carefully, she discovered tiny footprints in the snow. Quickening her pace, she failed to see an exposed tree root that sent her tumbling face down into a patch of snow and mud. As the footprints faded out, she began to panic.

"Pamela, where are you?" Offering a silent prayer, she cried out for Pamela again. Not far away, she could hear the faint whimpering of a child.

"I'm coming!" she shouted, closing the distance between them. Under a tree, she found Pamela shivering, tears streaming down her face.

"Darling," Eliza picked her up and hugged her. "I've got you. You're safe." Pamela sobbed and clung to Eliza, their tears mingling with one another's.

"I couldn't see Papa, just big trees," Pamela managed to say. Holding her close, Eliza could feel Pamela shivering, from cold or fear or both.

"It's all right, Pamela. You're safe with me. We'll be back with your Papa very soon. Everything will be just fine."

"Do you know the way back to Papa?" Pamela asked between sobs.

"I do." Setting Pamela down and wiped her tear-stained face with her sleeve. Eliza explained, "I'm going to carry you piggyback. When I stoop down, crawl on my back and put your arms around my neck. Do you think you can do that?"

Pamela nodded that she could. With her in place, Eliza wound her way back through the myriad of trees. As they emerged into the clearing, Lily began ringing the bell.

"Oh, thank goodness you found her!" Lily cried tears of relief, kissing her niece on the forehead. She handed a blanket to Eliza. Shifting Pamela from her back, Eliza wrapped her in it, holding her close.

"Pamela!" Thomas shouted, emerging from the trees, lines of worry etched on his forehead, his jaw tense. His expression changed almost immediately upon taking Pamela in his arms, as if she might slip away.

"Where did you find her?" Thomas asked.

"Huddled under a tree." Eliza pointed toward the direction she had come from.

"I was looking for pine cones, and then I couldn't see you, Papa." Pamela trembled.

"When you are warm, my dear little Pamela, we'll find the finest pine cones in the forest," Thomas assured her.

She reached up and hugged her father. "I love you, Papa." She reached out her hand to Eliza. "I love 'Liza too." Witnessing such a tender scene brought tears to Eliza's eyes. Reaching into her coat pocket, she discovered she had lost her handkerchief. She felt something being slipped into the other hand, and realized it was Thomas's handkerchief.

"I'm most grateful to you, Miss Wentworth."

She stood, wiping her eyes. "Providence was with us. When I could no longer follow Pamela's footprints in the snow, I prayed for help. Then I heard her crying."

Thomas stood there in silence for several minutes. Then he removed a damp glove and reached up, brushing dry mud from her face. He spoke softly, "You have taken a fall. Are you all right?"

"Yes. I am well." This small, kind act affected Eliza. It was just a touch, nothing more, but it had sent shivers down her spine. She locked eyes with Thomas momentarily.

Looking down, Eliza noticed her spoiled coat. "What a sight I must be!" she exclaimed, and started brushing off mud.

"You have never looked lovelier," Thomas said in earnest.

Suddenly Daniel sprinted up. "I can't tell you the relief I felt when I heard the bell ringing. Lily told me you found Pamela, Miss Wentworth." Eyeing Eliza's disheveled appearance, he grinned. "Fortunately, the mud on your coat almost matches its brown color." They all laughed, breaking the tension that had arisen. Eliza attempted to brush more mud off her coat.

Thomas turned to Daniel and said, "This is the first time since her mother's death that Pamela has told anyone besides her grandmother and me that she loves them."

"Come on, you little imp," he continued, taking Pamela by the hand, "let's go find some pinecones." The rest of the party began loading the sleighs with their fresh-cut treasures. Despite their efforts to keep them in some order, branches protruded in every direction, sticking out of what looked like a misshapen tree.

Hitching the horses, the group headed back to the manor. Lily spontaneously began to sing Christmas carols. Soon they were singing Christmas carols such as "Here We Come A-Wassailing," and "I Saw Three Ships Come Sailing" accompanied by the rhythmic jingle of bells attached to the horses. The dampened mood was gone like dew on fresh morning grass.

Eliza enjoyed watching Pamela and Abigail trying to catch snowflakes on their tongues as snow began falling. Ned boasted that he was much too old for that, but soon joined in the fun. Then, it began snowing in earnest, with large heavy snowflakes dotting their coats like chunks of cotton.

It wasn't long before everyone was seated in the dining room, enjoying chicken soup, dumplings, and mulled cider. Thomas glanced over at Eliza, watching as she and Emmett enjoyed a lively conversation. Eliza was relaxed and happy, and laughed at Emmett's anecdotes. Meanwhile, Thomas tapped his fingers nervously on the table, his impatience evident until Admiral and Mrs. Saunders asked to be excused, prompting the others to follow.

Intending to go to her room, Eliza paused at the top of the staircase and looked at Julia's portrait, reflecting on the morning's fear over Pamela's disappearance. She wondered, if Julia had been alive and with them, Pamela might not have gotten lost. As glad as she was to return to Bentley Manor, she felt sorrow over the loss of her friend engulf her once more. She couldn't shake the uneasy feeling that the days ahead would be emotional and bring back bitter-sweet memories. Her mind wandered until Mrs. Adams made her presence known.

"Can I help you, Miss Wentworth?" Mrs. Adams asked as she placed a lovely spray of fresh flowers on a walnut table accented with decorative motifs.

"I was just thinking about my dear friend." Eliza struggled to control her tears. "I loved her like a sister."

"I remember how highly she always spoke of you," Mrs. Adams said. "So sad. Her life was cut short at such a young age. She was so lovely and kind, and was completely devoted to Lord Bentley and their children."

Eliza's earlier doubts resurfaced, causing her mind to race as she tried to concoct some reason for leaving. She was trying to convince herself that fleeing would be best and allow her to avoid the conflicting emotions she was having.

As if sensing her unease, Mrs. Adams said kindly, "If I may be so bold, miss, your presence here is like a ray of sunshine—just what we need, particularly because it's the holidays and Lord Bentley's return from a three-year absence."

Eliza could have hugged her. "Thank you, Mrs. Adams. I appreciate hearing that. I want to be helpful and cheerful, although there are times that are more difficult than others." Mrs. Adams gave a nod of understanding.

"I hear you found Pamela this morning," Mrs. Adams said.

"I didn't do it alone. I know Pamela was being watched over." Mrs. Adams smiled warmly, adjusting the flower arrangement one more time, and then continued on her way.

Deciding not to go to her bedchamber, Eliza strolled down the hallway, examining the new paintings that had been added. Pausing at the spacious library, she was drawn inside and began searching through the tall, floor-to-ceiling walnut bookcases. Tempted to climb the wooden ladder to reach the top shelf, she spotted a book she had been wanting to read: *The Leavenworth Case* by Anna Katharine Green, known for its strong female characters. Settled in one of the overstuffed leather chairs, she was lost in her own world until Thomas's voice broke the silence.

"Miss Wentworth." Startled, she dropped the book. Seeing the book on the floor he added, "I didn't mean to take you by surprise."

As they both leaned over to retrieve it, they found themselves nose to nose.

"I believe this is yours," Thomas said, extending the book, his eyes locked on hers.

"Thank you," she stammered, unnerved by their close proximity and intrigued by his dark brown eyes. She felt a mix of embarrassment and curiosity wash over as she gathered her wits about her.

"I'll return at a later time," she said, beginning to walk away.

"Nonsense. Please stay," Thomas insisted. "Daniel and I were just discussing a potential investment in Remington typewriters." He showed her the picture he was holding and explained the keyboard. She enjoyed listening to him, recalling Julia's remark that she could listen to Thomas talk on a variety of subjects.

"Well, enough about typewriters," Thomas said, placing the picture on a nearby end table. "Please sit down, and make yourself comfortable." He gestured to the chair she had been sitting in.

Eliza felt a mix of emotions as she found herself alone for the first time with her best friend's husband.

TETE-A-TETE

*E*liza had been in Thomas's company in the past, but had never entertained any romantic thoughts about him. Of course, it had been impossible not to notice his striking appearance and sophisticated manner. She had admired him from afar and was very aware of the gentlemanly demeanor. He had always treated Julia with respect.

Today, she noticed the scent of his musky cologne, and thought how well he looked in his tan waistcoat and perfectly-tied ascot. As she fidgeted, she tried to divert her thoughts elsewhere.

"Welcome back to the library," Thomas said, his eyes reflecting genuine pleasure. "I know this was always one of your favorite rooms. Please, make yourself at home, and feel free to take a book to read now or when you return home. If you're partial to mysteries, I think you'll find *The Leavenworth Case* very interesting."

"I do like mystery novels. When I was fourteen, I had a copy of *Revelations of a Lady Detective.* When my father discovered me reading it, he thought it was inappropriate and exchanged it for *The Secret Garden.* I loved the book, but it wasn't as intriguing as my mystery book." Thomas chuckled at her confession.

Eliza continued. "On one of my trips to London, I came across a copy of Florence Nightingale's *Notes on Nursing*. My fascination with medicine grew stronger, and I decided I wanted to become a nurse. When I presented the idea to my father, he wouldn't hear of it. He said that no daughter of his was going to be part of the working class, and it would not be necessary for me to earn money. Like all the other young ladies, I could learn all the practical skills I need to know from my mother."

"I suppose that was the end of that!" Thomas said, his gaze lingering on Eliza.

Eliza fidgeted with a sleeve under his gaze, then a memory sparked and she gave a mischievous grin. "Actually, it wasn't. I secretly went against my father's wishes."

"Bold move," Thomas said, leaning in and resting his chin on his hand. "Not many young women would have the confidence to do that."

"I convinced our local doctor, Dr. Dyer, that if he would give me some training, I could help him when he visited patients. I explained that my father was against me pursuing medicine. Fortunately, Dr. Dyer felt I should be able to make my own decision, and agreed to take me on. I have been careful not to visit acquaintances of my father. I don't want him to hear from someone else that I was helping Dr. Dyer. Perhaps someday my father will recognize my determination as being positive, rather than just being stubborn."

"I hope so, too. It has been my observation that it is rare to see a woman of your background giving such important service." Without realizing it, they were leaning closer to each other, finding common interests they had never realized before, most likely because they had never had a conversation between just the two of them. Such personal discussions of this nature would have been improper. They were always respectful of their situations, Thomas married, and Eliza an unmarried woman.

They spoke of past events. Thomas brought up the annual boat race held in 1884 between Cambridge and Oxford. "Julia and I had been married the summer before. Of course, we were rooting for

Cambridge, who won. Watching those rowers racing down the Thames River was impressive," remarked Thomas.

"I remember," Eliza said, "it was near the beginning of my second season in London and I was staying at my Aunt Elizabeth's. After the race, we walked to Fulham Palace Gardens with its majestic trees and lovely flower beds. Julia brought along a picnic, complete with scones, clotted cream and jam."

Thomas laughed. "We teased Daniel about his voracious appetite. He claimed he was a starving student."

"When the second season began, Julia was determined to introduce me to some notable single gentlemen," Eliza reminisced. "I remember the ball given by Lord and Lady Brewster. Julia was so eager to introduce me to Rand Brewster, their eldest son, she became tongue-tied and called him Band Rooster, instead. That was a precursor for the rest of the night. I soon discovered *Mr. Rooster* preferred talking about horses rather than dancing." Eliza's expression shifted slightly, reflecting traces of regret when she thought about her unexpected departure from London at her father's insistence to distance herself from a family in financial trouble.

Thomas skillfully changed the conversation to the family's move back to Amersham, settling into Bentley Manor, and how pleased he was to have returned. After three years of silence, their words flowed freely, like a cascade of water tumbling over rocks into a tranquil pool below.

"Leaving so suddenly for London after Julia's passing meant I didn't have the chance to speak with you or any of my friends. In hindsight, I wish I had. I'm certain it would have been consoling," Thomas admitted.

"But you had your parents," Eliza said.

"True, and I shall be forever grateful for their help. When I arrived in London, they assumed much of the care of Ned and Pamela. We were often invited to Julia's sister Laura's home. Their children, Madison and Megan, would take Ned and Pamela on nature walks, pushing Pamela in her pram while Ned collected pinecones and rocks. Mrs. Carol Noble, Julia's mother, loved doting on the children.

She taught Ned finger plays and nursery rhymes and knitted some little clothes for Pamela."

"They sound wonderful, so kind and helpful," Eliza remarked.

"They truly are. Incidentally, Mrs. Noble, as trustee of her late husband's estate, and in accordance with his wishes, has set up trusts funds for all her grandchildren, including Ned and Pamela. They will receive these funds when they turn eighteen." Eliza smiled. Her understanding of the law concerning trust funds was practically non-existent, but she was pleased to hear about them being set up for the children.

Thomas shifted in his chair. "Other than being with family, I went out very little. While my parents encouraged me to engage with friends and invited me to church services, I declined. One day, I noticed Ned losing interest in coming activities and Pamela was becoming fussy. She would cry over anything. It became clear that my moroseness was affecting my children and I couldn't allow that to continue." Thomas paused as he thought about those difficult times.

"Consequently," he continued, "the next Sunday I went to church. I was searching for help. The Pastor's sermon that morning was centered on Galatians 5:13, *By love serve one another.* After the services, I spoke with him, and discovered we shared a common bond of losing a close family member. He must have recognized some of the pain I was feeling, because he said that often guilt sets in as a result of wondering if more could have been done."

"But, none of us knew how ill Julia was. You even engaged Dr. Bradley Fitzroy, one of the finest doctors in London, to consult on the case. He even traveled to Amersham to see Julia when she was too weak to travel," Eliza said with conviction.

"True, but there were times when I was preoccupied with business dealings, even traveling to London on several occasions," Thomas admitted, a hint of guilt accompanying his words. "I have learned since, business can wait, but the care of family cannot."

Eliza noticed Thomas's hands clenched. A few tears slid down her cheeks. She looked momentarily flustered as she fumbled to find her own handkerchief, unsure whether it was in her purse or jacket. Thomas promptly handed her his handkerchief, which he kept in his top pocket. It bore the letter *B*, undoubtedly embroidered by Julia. Eliza accepted it, her fingers lightly brushing against his, and a look of understanding and compassion passed between them.

"The Pastor referred to his sermon on service, and encouraged me to reach out to others. He promised that serving others would help me heal."

"It's my understanding that you and Julia gave to a number of charities," Eliza said.

"True. But the Pastor was speaking of giving service in a more personal way. I was accustomed to being served rather than doing the serving," Thomas admitted.

"Was it difficult? I mean, to serve people you might not even know?" Eliza asked, recognizing that Thomas's navigating through the loss of Julia had been a much harder battle than she had realized.

"It was at first. It felt uncomfortable when I accompanied my father to visit Sir Herbert Middleton, a neighbor who had been injured in a fall. Sir Herbert reminded me of my grandfather Bentley, and before long we became friends. I believe he helped me more than I helped him."

"During this time, the Pastor would send me notes of encouragement with a scripture or two included. I found my faith again, and with it, I found peace. Instead of lamenting the past, I began looking forward to the future with hope, " Thomas said.

"Soon afterward, I started rejoining society, accepting dinner invitations, attending concerts, and most notably, attending church regularly."

"That must have felt good, being a part of things again," Eliza said.

"Indeed. It gave me a sense of normalcy. I was able to move forward, even though it was without my dear companion. I took the children on outings," he continued, "but soon learned they preferred drinking hot cocoa and peppermint from a street vendor than going to Buckingham Palace and riding down South Carriage Drive in Hyde Park."

Eliza stifled a laugh. "Children usually like simple things, especially if it involves food."

"While in London, one of the most difficult sights for me to witness was the streets lined with filth and orphaned children. It was terrible, but what really horrified me was that the children I saw on the street corners reminded me of my own children. No child should have to starve in the city street. In the future, I plan to advocate for bills in the House of Lords aimed at providing assistance for these vulnerable children."

"I am deeply touched by what you have shared, Lord Bentley," she murmured softly, her eyes still glistening from a few remaining tears.

"Other than my family, you are the only person I have spoken with about these things," he confided.

"Be assured, our conversation will remain private," she told him. "Have you been able to do any service since your return to Amersham?"

"Actually I have." Thomas shifted in his chair, resting his elbow on his knee, nearly touching hers. There was a mischievous glint in his eye.

Suddenly, she thought of the two men she had seen in town and a suspicious look crossed her face. Cocking her head to one side, she contemplated the connection.

"A week or so ago, I saw a man at the church loading supplies that reminded me of someone I knew. A few days prior, a man driving a wagon full of furniture, wearing a green plaid coat and navy cap, looked familiar. Now I'm thinking both times it was you," Eliza said, scrutinizing Thomas.

"And I thought I was being so clever," he chuckled. "I didn't wish to draw attention to myself. I just wanted to help without it being a topic of discussion around town. My motives could be misunderstood and possibly criticized. Unjustifiable, many people feel that it isn't proper for someone in my position to be doing manual work or helping in such a way. I think it is a pity that some social norms are dictated by what society expects of us."

"My lips are sealed." She ran a finger across her lips, recognizing his challenges weren't too different from hers, wanting to be trained in medicine and work with Dr. Dyer.

"Oh, I forgot to tell you, I recently became an aunt." Eliza beamed. "My sister, Margaret, and her husband have a new baby girl they named Victoria, in honor of Queen Victoria." Eliza became very animated talking about her niece, and her eyes lit up with excitement.

"They are coming for Christmas. Even though Victoria is only three months old, Mother has been frantically getting everything ready for her." Counting with her fingers she said, "We now have a cradle, blankets, a pram, little dresses with caps, baby booties, and a little doll, which Victoria won't be old enough to play with for months."

"With all the goings-on, I'm delighted you were able to come," Thomas replied. Embarrassed about prattling on so, she fidgeted with an errant strand of hair that had fallen on her face, pushing it back into place. Thomas regarded her with a look of genuine appreciation, his eyes reflecting the warmth he felt.

Suddenly, a light knock on the door interrupted the moment. "I beg your pardon, Lord Bentley, you are needed downstairs," a footman said.

"I'll be right there," Thomas responded reluctantly, assisting Eliza out of her chair. The awkwardness between them had disappeared, and the likelihood of their relationship evolving in a new way was on the horizon.

THAT EVENING the dining room was adorned with flickering candlelight that cast a warm glow on the rich wooden table. Crystal glasses and fine china were carefully arranged for each guest. The room was filled with the aroma of a splendidly prepared roasted ham, freshly baked bread, and other culinary delights.

Amid the gracious surroundings, Eliza was seated between Emmett and Thomas. There was a subtle yet undeniable sense of vying for her attention. Surprisingly, she found the situation rather flattering. Each time Thomas spoke of one of his experiences, Emmett would quickly counter with one of his. The friendly banter continued until Admiral Saunders spoke of his time at sea.

The night was enhanced with the arrival of Christmas carolers that included both adults and children. They warmly welcomed Lord Bentley's family back to Amersham. Clad in their nightwear and rubbing their eyes, Pamela, Ned, and Abigail were brought down from the nursery. Before long, they were excitedly passing out bags of candy to the visitors.

"It seems our little Pamela is morphing into being very comfortable around others," Daniel said, as he joined his brother.

"I couldn't be more pleased. Our move to Amersham agrees with her. You and your family have had a big part in that," Thomas said.

"And I believe Miss Wentworth has, too," Daniel added.

Both men smiled at Eliza, and she fidgeted with her sleeve. She felt flushed under their attention.

Especially Thomas's.

LOOMING CLOUDS OVERHEAD

*T*he next morning, the Great Room was filled with the hustle and bustle of those gathering around the tables of pine boughs and bare-branch wreaths begging to be decorated. The refreshing scent of pine enveloped Eliza, instantly awakening her senses. She was captivated by the grand Christmas tree in the center of the room, adorned with twinkling candles and elegant decorations of cream, pink, and cranberry hues. Pearls and feathers added an exquisite touch.

Thomas appeared at her elbow. "You seem quite fascinated with our Christmas tree."

"It is truly beautiful," Eliza said, "and quite a departure from the one at home. Ours boasts some lovely, elegant decorations, but this one is truly lovely."

"Julia bought these ornaments in London, but was never able to use them." Thomas suddenly got a faraway look on his face.

"She would have loved it," Eliza said. They gazed at each other, and she experienced the same feeling she'd had while in the library. Looking at Thomas, she believed he did as well.

"The tree is a sight to behold, Thomas," Emmett remarked as he walked up and joined them. There was the slightest twitch at the corner of Thomas's eye, and Eliza got the impression he wasn't pleased with Emmett's presence. She wondered why.

"I understand we are to decorate the evergreen wreaths that are on the tables," Emmett said. "I've spoken with Miss Saunders and she has offered to help with the designs. I've learned she is an accomplished artist, excelling in water colors. She modestly admitted she once considered a professional career in art, but because she faced significant obstacles being a woman, she decided to simply paint for family and friends."

"My talent is nothing of that nature," Eliza lamented, "but I'd be happy to help if you would like me to, Lord Bentley."

"Excellent. Well, Emmett," Thomas said, facing his cousin squarely, "perhaps we can make it a little more interesting and see who can create the most impressive wreath. I suggest we divide into three groups. Miss Saunders, Miss Wentworth, and Mrs. Bentley can be the leaders."

"Some have said I have a flair for such things," Emmett replied smugly.

"You've never decorated a wreath in your life," Thomas scoffed.

"When I was younger, I would help my mother," Emmett insisted.

Thomas raised an eyebrow. "By carrying boxes for her?"

"Please, gentlemen. We shall have a fair contest. You will both have the opportunity to prove your skill," Eliza grinned.

"Well, we shall see, Emmett. May the best wreath win," Thomas declared with a determined look in his eyes.

Breaking into the three groups, the wreath challenge began—each group setting out to create one with its own style and flair.

Ribbons, pinecones, small wooden ornaments, silver bells, flowers, bows, cinnamon sticks, and other assorted items were strewn along the tables. With Eliza's help, Pamela was pulling out the loops on red bows. Thomas and Emmett exchanged challenging looks several times. Soon, three very distinct wreaths were completed and ready to be judged.

Miss Saunders' group, which included Emmett, used silver bells attached by a variety of lace and pastel organza ribbons, with stars intermingled in a very intricate design. The addition of a few feathers gave the wreath a strikingly artistic look.

Thomas was part of Eliza's group. Their wreath was a more rustic wreath, with its charm coming from natural items—pine cones, cinnamon sticks, and cranberries. A lovely red bow, courtesy of Pamela, added the perfect finishing touch.

Along with Lily and Daniel, Ned had enthusiastically joined the third group in creating a wreath using wooden ornaments, miniature presents, glitter, and candy canes tucked here and there. A ribbon, designed with a snowflake on it, added a touch of wintery charm to their creation.

When Mrs. Adams came into the room along with two house-maids carrying trays of hot beverages and finger sandwiches, she was quickly recruited as the judge. After some deliberation, Mrs. Adams declared a three-way tie and determined each wreath would hang in a prominent place in the Great Room, remaining there throughout the season.

Exhausted from entertaining Pamela and trying to create a perfect wreath, Eliza sat down in a comfy, red velvet chair, sipping hot chocolate. She thought Thomas was eyeing the seat beside her, but Emmett quickly took the empty seat.

A strange sense of disappointment bubbled up inside Eliza, but she was nothing if not polite. "Mr. Bentley, I think both of our handi-work turned out quite nicely," she began, "I wonder who picked out the supplies we used? Surely there is a very creative person in Lord Bentley's employ."

"Undoubtedly so," Emmett said in an offhand manner. He leaned closer to her. "Thanks to you, Miss Wentworth, and of course, the two other ladies, some very lovely creations were made."

"Mr. Bentley, I think you give me too much credit. We worked as a team." She leaned back a little further in her chair. She was not immune to Emmett's attentiveness and his engaging persona. But she also did not want to overly encourage him.

"You have an artistic touch," he insisted. Their conversation was interrupted when Thomas expressed his thanks to all and cheers of "hear, hear" rang out.

Thomas then suggested they all move to the drawing room. He informed them that luncheon would be served in an hour. As Eliza passed him on her way to the drawing room, she said quietly to Thomas, "Thank you for the book you gave me."

By the expression on Emmett's face, her comment had piqued his interest. Eliza would have classed his glance at his cousin as somewhat suspicious and even a bit competitive. Then again, Thomas had much the same look for Emmett.

"Miss Wentworth, may I walk with you to the drawing room?" Emmett asked, offering his arm.

She considered saying no that it wasn't really necessary, wanting to appear aloof, especially with Thomas standing nearby. Then, thinking better of it, and respecting Emmett's gesture of friendliness, she said, "I do appreciate your thoughtfulness," and took his arm.

"It is my pleasure," he replied with satisfaction.

Looking slightly irritated, Thomas carried Pamela into the drawing room, Ned lagging behind, kicking a large pine cone like it was a ball. Emmett and Eliza followed. Daniel came after them and seemed to be chuckling about something, looking between Emmett and Thomas. But he wouldn't say what was so funny.

They enjoyed much conversation and entertainment, games and laughter, long into the afternoon. Later, as Eliza entered her bedchamber, the refreshing smell of pine enveloped her. Garland lined the mantle and wreaths with red bows were attached above the windows.

Now it seems like Christmas, Eliza thought with a smile. She settled down on the elegant chaise and immersed herself in her new book, eager to see if the mystery could be solved. Before long, she debated whether to take a nap or go for a walk. The allure of the outdoors won out. The cool air felt refreshing, but it was colder outside than she thought. She realized she had not dressed warmly enough, a habit she couldn't seem to overcome. In the future, she would need to work on balancing fashion with practicality.

Overhead, dark, thick clouds loomed like heavy drapes pulled closed to keep out the sunlight, turning it bitterly cold. Snowflakes began swirling in the wind, and she could feel a chill settle in. Hurrying back to her room, she heard branches outside the window making scratchy noises like the paws of an angry cat.

Peeking out the frosted window pane, she caught sight of Daisy scurrying to the servant's entrance, her cheeks flushed with excitement. Across the courtyard, Mr. Edwards made his way toward the stables, glancing back and waving.

"It's a shame," Eliza mumbled. "It seems they must be in love. But I know they must be meeting in secret because fraternization between servants of different households is highly discouraged. But they needn't hide from me. I certainly don't support that notion. Everyone should have the opportunity of marrying and having a family."

OUTSIDE, Thomas and Daniel made their way into the stable, finding Mr. Edwards busy brushing down one of the horses. He looked up, acknowledging their presence. "With the storm rolling in, it looks like the horses won't be getting much exercise tomorrow," he said.

"It certainly looks that way. Do we have plenty of hay and water?" Thomas asked, running his hand along the mare's mane.

"The stable hands brought in extra water from the well. We've plenty of hay and grass," Mr. Edwards replied.

"Good. Thank you, Mr. Edwards, for all your hard work. Our horses are in good hands." Thomas and Daniel exited the stable, battling against the fierce gusts of wind as they struggled to shut the heavy doors against the impending storm.

"I fear we're in for quite the blizzard," Thomas said, quickening his pace as thick-falling snowflakes clung to his coat. They hurried into the side entrance, providing shelter from the biting wind outside.

Once inside, Daniel asked nonchalantly, "How did your conversation in the library with Miss Wentworth go?" He stood knocking snow off the bottom of his boots.

"Actually, better than I could have imagined. In the past, I perceived her as a lovely, congenial young lady who was somewhat indulged, and rather frivolous. Now, I have a better idea of why she was so dear to Julia. Miss Wentworth has many fine qualities and has matured nicely these past three years."

"Hmm," Daniel grinned.

"What?" Thomas asked, wondering what his brother was inferring.

"Oh nothing, I'm just glad to hear things went well."

FESTIVITIES INTERRUPTED

"*D*aisy, are you all right?" Eliza asked, concerned about her. Standing in the doorway, Daisy's curly hair tumbled down like twisted strands of wet yarn.

"Come sit by the fire and I'll dry your hair." Eliza helped her disheveled lady's maid remove her coat. Working quickly, she dried and attempted to untangle Daisy's hair, which was no easy task. Her voluminous red curls were in complete disarray.

"Good heavens, how long have you been out in this storm?" Eliza asked, producing another towel, and ringing for an upstairs maid. When she arrived, Eliza requested ginger tea.

Still shivering, Daisy said, "Not for long, Miss Eliza. I was helpin' bring the potted plants outside into the foyer. They were already lookin' bedraggled with the snow and wind poundin' down on 'em."

As they sipped the ginger tea, Eliza tried to ignore the raspiness in her throat and the beginnings of a cough. "Daisy, I hate to admit this, but I got chilled outside. I just can't get sick. I refuse to!" Eliza shook her head in determination.

"Ah, sure, Miss Eliza, get yourself a good night's rest, some more tea, and you'll be fit as a fiddle."

That night at dinner, the weather was the main topic of conversation. The wind rattled the windows, and a cold draft crept into the room like an interloper, unsettling the guests. Outside, snow drifts sculpted into mounds like sand dunes added to the wintery scene. Inside, the crackling fire and gently hissing radiators offered some relief, but the persistent chill in the room reminded everyone of the winter's grip. To take their minds off the storm. Thomas announced that a delectable meal was ready.

"The dinner is positively a gourmet delight," Admiral Saunders declared once dinner was served. "Beef Wellington is one of my favorite dishes." When Mrs. Saunders nodded in agreement, the burgundy feather pinned in her hair bounced up and down. She appeared much younger than her distinguished-looking husband, who was graying at the temples.

"I've always wondered how it is prepared," Eliza said.

Emmett spoke up. "It's often served at my table. You know, it was named after the Duke of Wellington's victory over Napoleon."

"I think most of us are familiar with that piece of culinary history," Thomas said matter-of-factly.

The two men glared at each other and Eliza decided to try to break the tension in the room. "Lord Bentley, please compliment your cook and tell her how much we are enjoying the delicious meal," Eliza said. As he smiled and agreed to do so, Eliza's thoughts shifted from Beef Wellington to how striking Thomas looked in his dark brown waistcoat and cream-colored shirt. She was so distracted, she nearly toppled her delicate dessert cup of trifle. She wondered if he was as aware of her as she was of him.

After dinner, Thomas led the way to the drawing room, where two small tables were set up for cards. The room's off-white walls were softened by dark wood wainscoting and adorned with landscape paintings in gilded frames. Plush cushioned chairs were arranged on oriental rugs, offering comfortable seating.

Thomas began to approach Eliza, but Emmett promptly invited her to be his partner instead. Eliza found herself feeling a bit disappointed, but politely accepted Emmett's invitation, going to the table with him.

"I, for one, am grateful to be comfortably indoors where I can enjoy the company of friends and playing Whist," Daniel said, helping Lily with her chair as they joined Emmett and Eliza.

"As am I," agreed Admiral Saunders, guiding his wife and his daughter to their seats. Miss Saunders looked especially nice in a gown the color of a green meadow that almost matched the color of her eyes. Her light brown hair with streaks of golden highlights framed her face in soft waves. She smiled at Thomas as he joined them at the table. Thomas responded with a friendly smile, and immediately he and Miss Saunders were absorbed in conversation.

As Eliza glanced over at Miss Saunders at the card table, she became aware of the young lady's playful charm and the attention she was drawing, particularly from Thomas. For a brief moment, Eliza wondered if she had once been similar at Miss Saunders's age, full of youthful energy and delight in other's company and perhaps a touch flirtatious. A flicker of envy stirred within her—not just at Jane's exuberance, but at how Thomas seemed to be enjoying it. Perhaps it was part of being a good host. Immediately, brushing those feelings aside, she focused on the game and was more attentive to Emmett, who appeared genuinely interested in her, and made every effort to impress her.

Whist proved to be a perfect diversion, with the four sets of partners clearly enjoying themselves. Outside, the howling wind and the groaning trees provided a drastic contrast to the lively discussions and enjoyable activity within.

"You must come visit us, Lord Bentley," Mrs. Saunders suddenly declared, much to Eliza's quiet horror. "Then you can see some of the treasures my husband brought back with him from the wars. The shells he collected while in the Galapagos Islands are truly unique."

"Yes, you must," Miss Saunders added. "He had some thrilling and intriguing adventures while he was there. One of them involved him being surrounded by sharks while swimming in the ocean and having to carefully make his way to the shore walking between them."

"Oh my," Thomas said, "I must come over and hear more about this."

Eliza had to stop her mouth from gaping. *Go to the Saunders' house? Surely not!* But then, she also had to wonder why she minded so much.

"Admiral Sanders, you have certainly seen more of the world than most people have. I have only read about such exotic places," Thomas said with genuine interest. "Once the children are older, I want to take them traveling. I think it's important for their education."

Eliza was intrigued by Thomas's plans for such travel. As she listened, she couldn't help but reflect on her own limited experiences —just a few trips to London and a childhood visit to Brighton. She wished she could have seen more of the world, but such travel had been rare among her childhood friends.

As the evening continued, the Saunders' eventually excused themselves, followed by Daniel and Lily. Unexpectedly, Eliza was alone with Emmett and Thomas. The three settled into a strained, drawn-out silence. The lively conversation that once filled the room had faded, and was replaced by awkwardness.

The strange quiet was finally getting too much for Eliza, and she started to speak. "How are—?"

Miss Saunders popped back into the room, interrupting Eliza. "My father is having difficulty negotiating the stairs. Could I prevail on one of you gentlemen to help me?"

"Of course," Emmett volunteered, as he was seated closest to the door.

"Perhaps your parents would be more comfortable being on the main floor, Miss Saunders. Tomorrow I will see to it," Thomas said.

"Thank you, Lord Bentley," she replied with a coy smile. "My father does best if he doesn't have to climb stairs. He doesn't want to be a bother, and tries not to complain."

"I assure you, it is no bother," Thomas said kindly. "Please let me know if there is anything else I can do for you or your parents."

"I will," she responded, beginning to leave the room. She cast a fleeting glance at Thomas. Emmett followed behind and remarked, "She certainly is a thoughtful daughter to her parents. "

"They are very fortunate," Thomas agreed. Eliza nodded but felt unsettled by Miss Saunders's flirtatious behavior. Surely Thomas saw that she was much too young for him.

She realized she was having uncharitable thoughts and decided she should retire for the night. She was also beginning to feel a bit unwell. As Eliza prepared to leave, Thomas walked over to a mahogany end table, pulled out a magazine, and handed it to her.

"*The Lady's Pictorial.*" Her eyes lit up as she began scanning through the pages. "I love this magazine," she said. "I appreciate all the fashions, stories, and practical domestic advice for women."

"I saw this in London and recalled how much you and Julia enjoyed discussing the newest designs, especially those from Paris," Thomas remarked.

"How considerate of you!" Eliza replied, her smile bright even though she was developing a headache and scratchy throat.

"One more thing," he said, handing her a book.

Eliza took it, reading the cover. "*King Solomon's Mines*—a novel written by Sir H. Rider Haggard, based on his explorations in Africa. It sounds very interesting, Lord Bentley. Thank you. I know very little about Africa."

She thought back on Thomas's earlier remarks on traveling with his children. It would be a wonderful opportunity for them to experience new places. Perhaps one day, she could find herself exploring the world beyond her familiar surroundings.

With the exception of her father, she had not felt this valued for a very long time.

A NIGHT OF PERIL

*I*n her bedchamber at last, Eliza kicked off her shoes and removed her jewelry. Why had she stayed up so late in spite of a throbbing headache and various aches and pains? The motivation, she recognized, was her desire to not appear sick or miss out on anything. Soon the headache powder she had mixed in tea would take effect. Daisy unpinned and brushed her hair, long brown locks that cascaded down her back. Eliza couldn't wait to crawl into bed.

Suddenly, there was a loud pounding on the manor's front doors. The urgent banging echoed throughout the house. Slipping a wrapper over her pink silk nightgown and stepping into soft leather slippers, she quickly grabbed a ribbon and tied her hair back as she hurried to see what was happening.

"Blast, who can that be? Who in the dickens would be out in a storm like this?" Thomas's voice echoed in the grand hallway.

Quickly descending the stairs, Eliza held back a bit behind Thomas and Kingsley. When the doors were thrown open, there stood a half-frozen man clutching a shivering child, whose pale face was barely visible beneath the blanket wrapped around them.

"Help! Please help me. My missus and my son are trapped out in the snow," the stranger cried, breathless and desperate. Behind him was a weather-beaten horse, snorting.

"Come in, man, and tell us what has happened," Thomas said, drawing him inside.

Forgetting about her own discomfort, Eliza stepped forward. "May I take your child?" she asked.

"Miss Wentworth has medical training, and knows what to do," Thomas spoke with confidence. "What is your child's name?"

"Rosie. Her name is Rosie," he said as he handed his daughter to Eliza.

Eliza spoke in hushed tones. "Lord Bentley, this man has been exposed to the cold for a considerable amount of time. He must remove his wet clothing immediately and drink warm tea. I will take Rosie to the sitting room." Thomas nodded.

THOMAS AND KINGSLEY took the man's coat, while Mrs. Adams appeared with a thick, woolen blanket that was draped over the stranger's shoulders.

"Mrs. Adams, have a footman fetch Daniel and Mr. Edwards at once. Please tell them it is an emergency, and have tea taken to the parlor," Thomas said as he guided the unsteady man to where he could sit.

"Tell me what has happened, Mister...?" Thomas paused, waiting for the man's reply.

"Sutton. The name's Sutton." As he took a few sips of tea he explained, "We were heading to my sister's place, when our driver got sick, so we left him in Amersham. I took the reins, but the storm hit, and the road turned treacherous. The coach slid into a snowbank, nearly hitting a tree. I left my wife and son with the coach, wrapped in a couple of blankets, and told them to move around and stay close to keep warm."

"Do you have any idea where the coach is?" Thomas asked urgently.

"I think about two miles from here," Mr. Sutton replied. "I tied my wife's red scarf to a tree near a stone wall. Then I followed a fence that didn't lead me right here, but close enough to see the lights. I need to get back before they freeze to death. Can I take one of your horses?"

"Mr. Sutton," Thomas said, alarmed. "You must stay here and get warm. I'll form a search party. We'll leave immediately."

"But I promised I'd be back," Mr. Sutton protested.

"My stable master and brother will go with me. We know the countryside and you need to stay here with your daughter," Thomas urged, showing signs of agitation as time slipped away.

"Where is she?" Mr. Sutton began to panic.

Thomas quickly led Mr. Sutton to the sitting room, where Rosie lay on the settee in one of Pamela's nightgowns, wrapped in a down quilt. Eliza and Daisy tenderly held her tiny hands, dipping them in bowls of warm water, while a housemaid gently rubbed Rosie's feet and legs.

"Oh no." Mr. Sutton's face tightened with concern. "She's got frostbite! I was afraid to leave her with the coach, not sure how long it would be before help arrived."

"You did what you thought was best." Thomas reassured him, attempting to calm the man though his anxiety grew. "You brought her to safety, where she's getting excellent care."

Eliza looked up. "Rosie's going to be alright. She's doing well."

"Now we need to focus on finding your wife and son," Thomas stated in a firm, but kind tone. "You go with Kingsley, my butler, and he will get you into some dry clothes." He practically pushed him toward the staircase as Kingsley took over.

"I'll be praying for you," Mr. Sutton shouted as he was led away.

Emmett rushed up to Thomas. "I just heard about the Suttons. What can I do to help?"

"Mr. Sutton has agreed to stay here while I lead a search party. Will you go to the second floor and keep him as calm and comfortable as possible?"

"I will, Thomas. Godspeed." Emmett said.

Thomas walked out into the hall as Daniel appeared, looking tense. "What's happened?" he asked. Thomas quickly explained.

"How terrible," Daniel said, his eyes wide with concern. " I can't imagine if my wife were out there. Do you have a plan for their rescue?"

"I'm hoping you and Mr. Edwards will come with me. We need to leave as soon as possible."

"I'll be ready in a few minutes," Daniel said, bounding up the staircase, two stairs at a time.

"I'm told there is a family trapped out there in the snow, Lord Bentley," Mr. Edwards, the stable master, said, brushing off his coat. His hair was disheveled, a few strands clinging to his forehead, and his eyes bore the traces of sleep.

"A man named Mr. Sutton arrived in a panic, asking for help. His wife and son are stuck in their coach in the storm. Daniel and I are getting ready to search for them, and we need your knowledge of the countryside and your practical skills, which far exceed ours. Frankly, I don't think we can find them without your help."

"Of course," Mr. Edwards replied without hesitation. "I'll get the horses ready."

Thomas was relieved. "Thank you, Mr. Edwards. I knew I could count on you. Please bring our fastest and strongest horses, and put blankets on them. Also, get the waterproof coats from the stable hands and put them in the saddlebags."

"Yes, sir," Mr. Edwards replied before heading to the stables.

Thomas's valet quickly dressed him in thick socks, heavy boots, and leather leggings that strapped from the ankle to the knee. He grabbed a wool coat, scarf, and wide-brimmed hat. As Thomas entered the kitchen, he nearly stepped on a piece of oilcloth containing gloves, scarves, and a fleece blanket, which Mrs. Adams was tying into a bundle.

"There, that will keep everything dry," Mrs. Adams said with satisfaction. Jane Saunders had joined the effort, filling flasks with hot tea to pack in the saddlebags.

"I hope they find them in time," Jane fretted, securing the cap on the last flask.

"I'm sure they will," Mrs. Adams responded confidently. "These men are not only strong and capable, but also carry a steadfast faith."

The front doors stood open, revealing Mr. Edwards standing outside, securing the horses. The steam billowing from the horses' nostrils made them look as imposing as dragons. The sleek muscles beneath their coats twitched with anticipation, and their hooves pawed the ground. Snow swirling painted a dramatic background.

While Thomas adjusted his hat, Eliza came padding up in her slippers, her steps soft and quiet. He was unaware of her presence until she reached out and gently touched his cheek.

"Please be careful, Lord Bentley," she said softly.

"I will," he replied, instinctively covering her hand with his. Her show of concern warmed him, lending him strength as he prepared himself for the dangerous journey ahead. Releasing her hand, he stepped out into the storm.

A RACE AGAINST NATURE

*T*he riders had been trodding along for over an hour, although it seemed much longer. Despite the horses being fitted with horseshoes with sturdy cleats on the bottom, heavy clumps of snow were clinging to their hooves. Snow continued to swirl around them, as if it was challenging them to intrude into its domain. The frigid air tried to poke through their heavy coats, but, luckily, with little success.

"Look for a red scarf tied to a branch," Thomas shouted over the whistling wind. "Mr. Edwards, do you think we're heading the right way?"

"Yes. I just saw the sign pointing to Amersham. But I think we had better slow our pace so the horses don't get too tired." The three riders, their coats splattered with snow, slowed down. After trudging along for some time, Thomas reached into his saddlebag and pulled out a pair of binoculars.

"Binoculars?" Daniel exclaimed in amazement. "I've only read about them. Thomas, you're always one of the first with new inventions. Do they really work?"

"See for yourself," Thomas replied, handing them to him. "Do you see any signs of the coach?"

"I can't see very far with all this falling snow," Daniel confessed solemnly. "What if we're too late, and they freeze to death? All I see is snow and a few fence posts."

"I know it seems impossible, but we'll find them," Thomas replied with conviction. He held up his lantern and shone it on a fence post. "Mr. Edwards, does this look like the fence Mr. Sutton described?"

Mr. Edwards nodded. "It must be."

Thomas peered through the binoculars, straining to see farther. "We must be getting close," he said, spurring his horse onward. The three riders rode on in silence, their eyes the only visible feature above the wool scarves. Driven by the anticipation of reaching the stranded coach, they pressed ahead, with the horses breathing hard through the relentless snow.

Thomas halted once more, handing the binoculars to Mr. Edwards. "Can you see the red scarf or the big tree?"

Mr. Edwards scanned the landscape, straining his eyes in the moonless night. Visibility remained limited, shadows and snow merging into a ghostly scene. He shook his head. "No, I don't see either one. Or the coach, either."

Thomas felt his hope waning. He wondered how much longer they could continue to push the horses, and still find the Suttons in the dark. To his amazement, the snow stopped falling, leaving its calling card of drifts and inches of powder. The moon made an attempt to break through overhead. As the clouds parted slightly, it cast a faint light over the surrounding landscape.

"Wait—" Mr. Edwards said, his voice filled with excitement. "I can see the red scarf!" A sliver of moonlight cut its way through the clouds, reflecting off the snow like a beacon in the night, lighting the way.

Urging the horses on, the three men were able to make out the silhouette of a coach. Dismounting, and fearing what they might find, they approached the coach's door and opened it. Inside, huddled in one corner of the seat, were Mrs. Sutton and her son.

❄

Rosie was sleeping peacefully now.

"Miss Wentworth, you must be tired from your vigilance over Rosie. If you would like to sit for a bit, there's tea in the breakfast room," Mrs. Adams said, urging Eliza to take respite.

"That sounds wonderful." Eliza was hoping it would help cure her throbbing headache and ease her unsettled feelings. She felt secure leaving Daisy, who was dozing on and off, sitting in a rocking chair by the sleeping child.

"They've been gone for over two hours," Eliza fretted. "Do you think something's happened to them?" she asked Mrs. Adams.

"It'll be slow going, miss. Rest yourself and I'll inform you the minute they arrive."

Sipping tea while trying to stay awake, Eliza realized how much she needed rest. Barely able to keep her eyes open, she waited anxiously. When she had just closed her eyes, she felt someone taking hold of her hands, rousing her.

"They're here," Mrs. Adams announced with relief in her voice. There was quite a hubbub in the entryway.

"You're safe, my dear. You're safe," Mr. Sutton said, springing from the bench where he had been waiting in the hallway. Mrs. Sutton fell, weeping, into her husband's arms.

"Will." Mr. Sutton could say no more, embracing his son, who was almost as tall as his father.

"Rosie, where is my Rosie?" Mrs. Sutton asked frantically.

"I'll take you to her, dear," her husband said as she and Will shed their waterproof coats and headed to the sitting room. There was a flood of emotion as Mrs. Sutton, Mr. Sutton, and Will entered. Rosie began to stir and looked up at her parents, smiled, and then fell back asleep.

Eliza hurriedly made her way into the grand hall. The sight of Thomas was surreal. Despite the hat he had been wearing, his hair was damp, and his wet coat and gloves lay discarded on the floor. The sight of him—alive and safe—was a profound relief.

Eliza was overwhelmed by a surge of comfort and gratitude. She felt an urgent need to touch him, to reassure herself of his presence.

The worry she had endured and the fear of losing him, along with the devastating effect this would have on his children, was almost too painful to bear. She put her arms around him, closed her eyes, and wondered if she might be dreaming. When he wrapped his arms around her, she knew this was no dream.

"Miss Wentworth," he said gently, holding her close. She felt a sense of relief and her feelings for him became undeniable.

"The longer you were gone, the more I worried about you," she admitted.

Thomas responded in a serious tone, "I couldn't endure the thought of my children being fatherless. Of course, finding the Suttons was paramount. But I kept thinking about you—standing at the door when I left. That meant everything to me, to know you truly cared about my well-being."

Then he added, with a slight chuckle, as he tilted her chin up with the tips of his fingers, "Besides, I wasn't about to miss a greeting like this."

With a self-conscious realization, Eliza stepped back but did not apologize. Noting the melting snow dripping from his under-jacket, she pointed toward the staircase. "Lord Bentley, you must get out of these wet clothes immediately!"

"Yes, ma'am," he said, raising an eyebrow as he started to walk away. "Really, how preposterous—being bossed around in my own household," he teased, then muttered under his breath, "I rather enjoy it."

Upon entering the sitting room, Eliza was relieved to see Mrs. Sutton, wrapped in a blanket, singing softly to Rosie.

"You must be Miss Wentworth," she reached out her hand and took Eliza's hand. "Mrs. Adams has told me how you and Daisy have cared for my dear little Rosie. I am so grateful to you both."

"Seeing your family safe and together is reward enough," Eliza said, looking at Mrs. Sutton's hand. "You have no frostbite. That is wonderful."

"Fortunately our coach has glass windows and we were able to stay relatively warm wrapped in blankets, but Will insisted we move about. Lord Bentley said my red scarf led them to us. It was a miracle!"

Then Mrs. Sutton exclaimed. "I don't think I have ever prayed harder in my life!"

Eliza smiled and replied, "We were praying for you, too. We were praying for the rescuers. I hope you know there were people who cared about you, even if you hadn't met them." Speaking of such tender matters, Eliza wiped away a tear or two and stepped out of the room, giving the door a gentle push to close it behind her. She took a moment to compose herself before heading to the stairway.

At the bottom of the staircase, leaning against the stair post, stood Thomas, dressed in a navy sweater and gray wool trousers. After experiencing such an ordeal, he looked remarkably handsome and composed. He must have made an effort to change quickly and return downstairs. *Why is Lord Bentley back?* she wondered. Was it to check on the Suttons, or was he concerned about her? As she walked towards him, her steps became unsteady.

"Miss Wentworth, let me help you," Thomas said, taking her arm. As they ascended the staircase, she leaned into him, mumbling incoherent words, and beginning to falter. Her face brushed against his, and he could feel the warmth radiating from her feverish skin. Realizing she wasn't well, he quickly scooped her up into his arms, her head nestled against his shoulder. Carrying her with a protective tenderness, Eliza began to drift off, succumbing to sleep.

Entering her bedchamber, Thomas gently placed her on the bed, Eliza's hair spreading across the pillow, framing her face. Thomas thought she looked both lovely and vulnerable. He thought of the remarkable strength she had shown during the night that was crucial to its being successful. The medical skills she had told him about proved vital in the treatment of little Rosie. Most touching was the concern she had for him.

"Whatever happened, my lord?" Daisy rushed over to Eliza's

bedside. She had been sitting in one of the chairs, waiting for Eliza to return, and had fallen asleep.

"She fainted, most likely from exhaustion, and has a slight fever. Take care of her, Daisy, and please don't hesitate to ring if you need anything," Thomas instructed. "I would stay and watch over her, but that would be improper."

"Don't worry, sir, I'll be takin' good care of her," Daisy said, beginning to remove Eliza's slippers. "If I need 'elp, I'll send for it."

"Thank you, Daisy. I have every confidence in you. She couldn't ask for a more devoted lady's maid." Daisy blushed and nodded in appreciation.

Thomas's heartbeat quickened as he leaned down close to Eliza and whispered, "Well done, brave warrior."

EMBRACING CALM AFTER THE STORM

*T*he next morning, Eliza woke up feeling disoriented. As she blinked, she wondered where she was. In her own room? In someone else's room? She didn't even recall going to bed. Her memory, hazy from the night before, slowly began coming back to her.

"Ah, sure and it's awake you are," Daisy said cheerfully.

Glancing at the clock on the mantle, Eliza gasped, "I can't believe I slept this late! It's almost noon." Leaning over and pulling the curtain aside, she expected to see the sun high in the sky. Instead, she was greeted with a sight both serene and surreal. The sun, caught between two stubborn clouds, struggled to make its appearance. Shadows of sculptured shapes appeared here and there over the snow-covered ground, as if the entire estate had been wrapped in a soft, icy embrace. The only disturbance in the wintry stillness was a myriad of horse tracks leading in and out of the stables.

Replacing the curtain she asked, "Daisy, how is everyone fairing this morning? Is Lord Bentley up and about?"

"Ah, yes, Miss Eliza. Lord Bentley is outside with the stable hands clearin' pathways around the manor," Daisy replied.

Eliza nodded, then spoke with a slight tremor in her voice. "I was very distraught last night. I think the memory of the terrible blizzard of 1881 added to my fear. I can still remember mounds of snow in front of our home. Father told me there were drifts in London as high as three feet, and hundreds of miles of train tracks were blocked by drifting snow. Many people died. The thoughts of something like that happening here was frightening."

"Have you heard how the Suttons are?" Eliza continued.

"They are all recoverin' nicely, and plan on leavin' tomorrow."

"I'm trying to remember what happened after I left the Sutton family," Eliza said with a sigh.

"Ye fainted, and Lord Bentley carried ye to your room," Daisy explained. "He was very worried about you, bless his heart. He even said he would stay, but it's not proper."

"Oh, my!" was all the reply Eliza could manage. Thoughts of him carrying her were very humbling. Her self-sufficiency had never required that before. "I don't want him to think I'm one of those swoony types. You know, women in corsets that swoon over the slightest stress or a nod from a handsome man."

"I dinnae believe he thinks that. He was aware ye were feverish and weary. I'm sure he knows the strength in ye, even if he might not have spoken it. Lord Bentley's seen how much you've done."

Eliza surveyed her reflection in the intricately carved stand-up mirror adorned with floral patterns. Upon closer inspection, she determined that she looked a little pale and decided that a touch of pink rouge on her cheeks would brighten her appearance.

"I want to dress in something simple today, Daisy. My cotton-flannel tea gown should do, and I will forgo crinolines. What do you think about pulling back some hair with combs and leaving the rest hanging loose?" Daisy nodded in agreement. With Daisy's help, Eliza was soon dressed and prepared for the day. Just as the last silver comb was placed in her hair, a maid appeared at the door with breakfast. Sipping her tea and eating an egg and biscuit, Eliza felt her strength returning. She made a mental note to ask Mrs. Adams where the fresh mint for the tea came from.

Venturing downstairs, she heard the laughter of children from the

Great Room. Pamela, Abigail and Rosie were being chased by Daniel. Giggles filled the air as he hid behind a curtain and then popped out and scared them. They squealed with delight, running to Lily for safety.

"Good morning, Miss Wentworth," Lily greeted her cheerfully. "I am glad to see you this morning. We were all concerned about you last night, especially Lord Bentley. Here, come sit by me." She patted the cushion next to her. Eliza appreciated the chance for a more personal conversation with Lily. Eliza had a positive impression of her, seeing Lily as someone she would like to know better.

"Good morning. Things seem much more normal today. Daisy told me Lord Bentley is outside while they clear the pathways. Where is everybody else, Mrs. Bentley?" Eliza queried.

"Oh, please call me Lily. May I call you by your Christian name?"

"I would like that." Eliza smiled.

"Thomas is coordinating with the stable hands, helping clear the pathways and Will Sutton is out helping."

"I'm surprised that Lord Bentley is so personally involved with the upkeep of the manor. Clearing the pathways with poles and sawdust is no easy task. He doesn't seem to mind doing some physical work himself," Eliza said.

"He likes to be involved with every aspect, and works closely with Mr. Harrison, his steward, as well as Kingsley. Sometimes, Daniel helps Thomas, too. Right now, Daniel is keeping the children busy. Not only are Daniel and Thomas brothers, but they are also best friends," Lily responded with pleasure.

"My sister Margaret and I are also close," Eliza revealed. "We had such fun growing up. By the way, Margaret and her family are coming for Christmas."

"How nice for you. I'm an only child," Lily said. "Daniel and I want Abigail to have the joy of growing up with brothers and sisters, experiencing the closeness of family bonds. As for us, we remain patient, hopeful for the day when our family can expand." Eliza smiled with a look of understanding. Lily continued her narrative of the morning's activities, explaining that Thomas had seen Dr. Dyer traveling by sleigh. Because of the storm, he had spent the night at a neighbor's house.

"Although he was anxious to return home, Dr. Dyer came in briefly to check on the Sutton family. After hearing the ordeal they had been through, he advised they rest today and delay traveling until tomorrow. Dr. Dyer peeked in on you, and found you were sleeping comfortably. He advised that you have a quiet day inside as well. Dr. Dyer was amazed at the daring rescue and spoke highly of the rescue party, as well as of your actions. He wasn't a bit surprised you were able to take care of Rosie," Lily concluded.

"I have read a few books on medicine, but it is a different matter when you have to actually apply that knowledge." Eliza was unwilling to share that she had worked with Dr. Dyer.

Just then, Rosie ran by, squealing and bouncing a ball. "Apparently, not all the Suttons need rest," Lily laughed. Eliza watched Rosie scamper away, amazed at her vibrance and energy. Pamela and Abigail followed closely behind, with Daniel bringing up the rear. As he approached, Daniel gave a theatrical wave to his wife and Eliza, before pretending to trudge away with exaggerated exhaustion.

"I think you can make it, dear," Lily said, smiling and waving back at her husband. Turning to face Eliza, she continued, "Now, what were we speaking of?"

"You were telling me about recent events. What about the abandoned coach?" Eliza asked.

"It is yet to be pulled out of the snow. Thomas thought it more practical to wait a day or two until some of the snow has melted. When the Suttons arrive at their destination, they will have their family retrieve the coach. For now, Thomas plans to have them travel in one of the sleighs here at the manor."

"Where are the others?" Eliza asked.

"Mr. and Mrs. Sutton, the Saunders family, and Emmett are gathered in the sitting room," Lily explained. "Emmett announced that he would stay indoors and mingle with them, and reiterated he won't do anything that would typically be done by servants." Lily's annoyance was clear.

Eliza acknowledged Lily's comment with a nod. "It's evident that not everyone shares that view. I think Lord Bentley and your husband are exceptional." Lily responded with a grateful smile.

"Well, I feel a need to join the others in the sitting room to see how the Suttons are doing," Eliza announced. "I'm so glad we have had this chance to talk, Lily, and hope we can again." She looked over and saw Ned on the other side of the room, sitting alone.

"Ned doesn't look very happy," Eliza observed.

"He wanted to be outside with his father." Lily confided, her voice tinged with a bit of sorrow. "But he has to remain indoors because of the hazardous conditions of snow removal. He is feeling the absence of his father, especially now since they have been spending so much time together."

"Perhaps I can do something to cheer him up. At least, I would like to try." Eliza decided to forgo going to the sitting room, and took a seat beside Ned.

"Ned, how are you today?" Ned just nodded, not uttering a word.

"Ned, I need your help. I've been told to spend the day indoors, and I am trying to think of something to do. Would you happen to have any board or card games?"

Ned suddenly became animated. "I have Checkers and Snap."

"I would love to learn how to play Snap," Eliza said with enthusiasm. Soon, she and Ned were grabbing up pairs and shouting, "Snap!" Between games, Ned shared how much he wanted to learn how to play marbles, and hoped he would get some for Christmas. Eliza asked about what else he liked to do.

"I like to ride horses and draw," he responded eagerly.

"What things do you like to draw?"

"Real animals like the ones Father reads about to me in storybooks like *The Swiss Family Robinson.* Sometimes I draw elephants and tigers."

"That sounds very interesting. I've brought something for you, Pamela, and Abigail to do later that involves drawing. I think you will like it, Ned." He grinned and took the last two cards off the pile.

"You've won again! If I want to beat you, I'm going to have to speed up picking pairs." Eliza smiled with a twinkle in her eyes.

Pamela, Abigail, and Rosie, worn out from being chased, sauntered over. "Ned. Can we play? Pwetty pwease," Pamela begged, giving her brother an adoring smile too pretty to resist.

Ned liked being in charge, and hurried off, promising he would get a game they would like. He quickly returned with the card game, Noah's Ark Animals. They played their own version, collecting a Mr. and Mrs. and baby animal of each species.

"I won!" Pamela squealed, tossing her cards in the air.

"What have we here?" Thomas asked, picking up one of the cards. He had walked into the Great Room unobserved.

Startled by the sound of his unmistakable deep voice, Eliza looked up, her heart warming at the sight of him. His cheeks were red, despite the herringbone scarf that hung loosely around his neck, and his hair tousled. Peeling off his winter gear, his beige shirt tails hung loosely over his trousers. Eliza was glad the card game was over. It would have been impossible for her to concentrate with him close by, looking so ruggedly handsome.

"And how are you today, Miss Wentworth?" Thomas bent over and looked at her closely to check for himself.

"I am well, thank you," Eliza replied warmly, though she was momentarily unsettled by his sudden presence. "As you can see, I'm enjoying playing games with Ned, Pamela, Rosie, and Abigail."

Ned spoke right up. "Papa, Miss Wentworth and I played Snap and I won."

"Wait until next time," Eliza laughed, wagging a finger at him.

Just then they were interrupted by Lily's announcement, "Would anyone like freshly baked cookies?" The news worked like a magnet, propelling the little girls in the direction of the dining room.

"Would you care to join Ned and me, Lord Bentley?" Eliza asked. Seeing the look of anticipation on his son's face, Thomas agreed to play. Ned dashed off as quickly as a jack rabbit running from its pursuer to the game cupboard.

"I haven't seen him this excited about something since coming to

Amersham. How do you do it, Miss Wentworth?" Thomas stretched out his legs and clasped his hands behind his head, clearly enjoying relaxing after a strenuous morning.

"I am not certain what you mean."

"Connect with the children so easily?" he clarified, arching an eyebrow.

"I like spending time with them, and trying to find out what they like to do. Once I discovered that Ned likes games, we were soon talking and enjoying the time together," she said. Feeling a little light-headed, she wondered if it was due to the strain of last night or Thomas's presence. Willing herself to breathe a little deeper and slower, the feeling passed.

"I am relieved that you are feeling better today," he said, squeezing her hand. "I was—" He paused. "—that is, we were all concerned about you."

"I don't remember anything after starting to climb the stairs," Eliza admitted. "Daisy told me you carried me to my room, which is so embarrassing. I've never fainted before in my life."

Thomas smiled. "Things happen. It was only then that I realized you were ill. Under such circumstances, you did amazingly well. I even called you a 'brave warrior.'" She blushed, delighted he felt she was strong.

The aroma of warm cookies diverted their attention as Ned returned with a trayful, as well as the game Little Jack Horner.

"This is a brand new game Papa got for us," Ned said.

"Here, Ned, let me open the box and read the rules." Laying cards on the table, Thomas explained, "We each collect cards of the same color to make a plum pie. Each color stands for a different part of the pie, and the first to gather all the pieces of their pie wins."

For the next while, there was much excitement as they learned to play the new game.

Then, Ned yawned.

"I think you look a little tired, Ned. It's time for you and the girls to have some quiet time in the nursery." Thomas stood, excused himself, and walked Ned to the door.

Eliza's thoughts felt scattered. Did she need a rest too from last night's exertion, or was it from being with Thomas? She convinced herself that fresh air would clear her mind and help her feel more steady. Walking into the entryway, she peeked out of a window and saw that a path had been cleared. It looked so inviting, and she thought, surely a few minutes outside wouldn't do any harm, and headed to her bedchamber for a cape.

GRANDMOTHER BENTLEY'S COZY CORNER

A woolen cape wrapped around her, Eliza stepped out of her bedchamber and made her way downstairs. With the children in the nursery, the house was unusually quiet. She slowly opened the entryway door.

Unexpectedly, a hand reached over her shoulder and gently shut the door. It was Thomas. "How thoughtful of you," he said tactfully. "Someone has left the door ajar, which would certainly create a draft. I wouldn't want you to become chilled."

"No, that wouldn't be good. I was just curious for a quick peek at the countryside," she said, displaying a charming smile, attempting to look innocent like a child who had just been caught with their hand in the cookie jar. Thomas, now dressed in more casual attire—a lightweight tweed suit and open collar shirt—seemed amused at her coy little look.

"I think I can help you with that." He offered her his arm and led her to the staircase. Just then, Emmett walked into the grand hallway, watching Thomas and Eliza climb the stairs. He had a disappointed look on his face.

Eliza frowned slightly in confusion, but was so absorbed by Thomas she soon turned back to him.

"Where are we going?" she asked Thomas.

"It's a surprise." He winked at her, clearly enjoying himself. They were now on the second floor, continuing to the third.

"Will you give me a hint?"

"Then it wouldn't be a surprise."

Arriving on the third floor, Thomas led Eliza down the hallway to the family's private quarters. Passing by the nursery, Thomas ushered her through an archway into a lovely room furnished with floral-patterned cushions adorning couches and chairs. Hand-woven rugs covered the hardwood floors. A small pot-bellied stove in one corner emitted a comfortable warmth, while fresh flowers graced a low round table in the center of the room.

"We call this room 'Grandmother's Cozy Corner.' This is where Grandmother Bentley would come and work on her stitchery, or enjoy private conversations with my grandfather or others. I have fond memories of coming here with Daniel and Emmett, listening to grand adventure stories that Grandmother would read to us while we enjoyed hot chocolate and gingerbread cookies. I thought you might appreciate the cozy ambiance and the panoramic view of the countryside," Thomas said with warmth in his voice.

"It's a delightful room. I can understand why your grandmother enjoyed her cozy corner." Making her way to the large bay window framed with delicate lace curtains, Eliza knelt on the inviting window seat, tucking her skirts beneath her. The countryside before her, blanketed in snow, caused her eyes to dance with excitement.

"I can see a few coach's tracks out there made by the few brave souls who have ventured outside," she said. "There's Hudson's Pond with homes nearby." Thomas smiled as he sat next to her.

"Does this satisfy your curiosity?" Thomas teased, taking her hand.

"I suppose," she said drolly, aware of how she was enjoying the pleasantness of his touch. "In truth, it is quite remarkable. Thank you for bringing me here."

"You seemed bent on seeing for yourself what the snow had done."

"My father has often said my determination could someday get me into trouble. Once I decide to do something, I have a difficult time stopping until it has been accomplished," she admitted.

"When properly applied, determination can also be a strength. It was your determination that led you to study medicine." She basked in pleasure hearing Thomas's words and would be content to sit there the rest of the afternoon.

Then, much to Eliza's delight, Thomas continued, "The view from here is undoubtedly breathtaking, but not as lovely as the one who sits beside me."

She blushed and turned to face him—their faces just inches apart. "Thank you for your kind words, Lord Bentley. I am enjoying being in your company as well." In the silent exchange of glances, they found a pleasurable connection that was now becoming more familiar to them.

Thomas pulled out his pocket watch and glanced at the time. "Dinner will soon be served. I need to inform everyone that they can forego formal dress and remain in their informal attire," he said.

As he helped Eliza off the window seat, she remarked, "I believe I hear children's laughter coming from the nursery. Do you want them to join us as we go downstairs?"

"That's a wonderful idea," Thomas replied. To the children's delight, Thomas and Eliza guided them out of the nursery, and they all continued downstairs together.

Dinner was served in an unhurried manner, buffet style with simpler tableware, stews, and pies. Next to the buffet was a table where a selection of drinks sat, including pitchers of water infused with herbs. Rustic baskets held a variety of breads. This setup encouraged guests to mingle and serve themselves, creating a relaxed atmosphere.

For after dinner entertainment, Thomas explained he had arranged to have a soiree that evening featuring a violinist and flutist he had hired in Amersham. However, given the circumstances of the storm, and the difficulty of travel, they never arrived.

The guests murmured a little of their disappointment, but perked up when it was then decided to have an impromptu soiree.

As Eliza entered the elegant music room, with its ornate furnishings and softly-lit flickering candles, she was suddenly overwhelmed by thoughts of Julia. She could picture her dear friend at the pianoforte, playing and singing one of her favorite melodies, the warm glow from the candelabra illuminating her lovely face. As Eliza's eyes welled with tears, Thomas walked up, handing her a handkerchief.

"Are you well?" he asked, gently taking her arm.

"I will be," she said, with a faraway look in her eyes. "I just experienced one of these unexpected moments when I felt the loss of Julia."

"I know just how you feel. In the past, as I have had poignant memories of Julia, I found them difficult to deal with. But with the passage of time, those memories have become more peaceful and comforting," Thomas empathized as he guided Eliza to a plush velvet armchair and sat beside her.

Jane was the first to play and delight her audience with several lively renditions on the pianoforte. Emmett, self-appointed soloist, then sang several ballads accompanied by Jane until his voice became strained.

Thomas began to doze off as Emmett kept ceaselessly singing. Eliza noticed his light breathing and him leaning back in his chair with his eyes closed. Reflecting on the events of the past two days and considering the effort he had put into the rescue and ensuring the safety of the manor, a deep sense of admiration brimmed within her. She recognized the strength of character and perseverance in the man sitting beside her, and how much she was beginning to care for him. The dichotomy of mourning her friend while developing feelings for Thomas was unsettling.

As Eliza slipped out of her chair to take her turn at the pianoforte, she nudged Thomas gently on his shoulder, discreetly placing a paper-wrapped mint into his hand. She whispered, "At my mother's suggestion, I always carry these with me. They help me stay awake." He responded with a warm smile.

Although less proficient than Miss Saunders, Eliza played Christmas carols well enough for a sing-along. Her father had encouraged her to learn to play, and tried to convince her that it would not only display a family's talent and wealth, but also attract a husband. She had stubbornly resisted most of the necessary practice for proficiency, and was certain her playing would not attract a husband.

The evening passed pleasantly, a welcome change from the drama of the night before.

A DELIGHTFUL DILEMMA

*a*s Eliza hugged Mrs. Sutton, she caught Thomas's muttered words, barely audible through the hum of conversation, "I do wish she wouldn't look so charming. It is positively maddening." Eliza blushed slightly, trying to act nonchalant.

"Miss Wentworth, you've been like an angel from heaven. Our hearts are knit in friendship," Mrs. Sutton said, her eyes tearing up. Eliza's emotions were too tender to reply, and she simply squeezed Mrs. Sutton's hand.

"Lord Bentley, not only did you save us, but you have treated us with such kindness. We are most grateful to you, your brother, Mr. Edwards, and the others for helping us in our time of need," Mrs. Sutton added to Thomas.

Thomas responded with a warm smile and a slight nod. "You and your family are always welcome at Bentley Manor."

Mr. Sutton, a man of few words, muttered his sincere appreciation. A sleigh with a driver had been prepared with extra blankets and a basket of refreshments. With a final wave, the Suttons bid farewell, and were on their way.

Thomas turned to Eliza, his lips parting to say something, when Mr. Harrison, his steward, interrupted, informing him there was a blockage in the heating system that needed his attention. Thomas excused himself.

Disappointed, Eliza went to busy herself elsewhere. The manor was unusually quiet with the departure of the Sutton family. Seeing Pamela's and Abigail's sad little faces at the loss of their new friend, Rosie, Eliza sprang into action. "Daisy, please fetch the gifts I brought for the children."

"Aye, I won't be long."

Minutes later, Daisy appeared with several packages. Eliza gave each girl a porcelain doll, and Ned a collection of tin soldiers. As Pamela and Abigail hugged her, Eliza was grateful she had purchased two dolls. Ned nodded his approval and rewarded her with one of his winning grins. Once the children were absorbed in their play, she decided it was time to take a walk outside. The weather was good enough, and her scratchy throat had finally cleared. There was no sign of Thomas, or anyone else to stop her, for that matter. A quiet moment alone sounded pleasant, as everyone else seemed to be off and busy.

Dressed in a royal blue ankle-length skirt and a matching tailored jacket, along with leather boots, she was well-prepared for mud or snow. Her fur-lined bonnet and leather gloves promised warmth. Though the weather was slowly improving and the temperature was rising, the air was still brisk.

As she strolled away from the manor, a familiar voice called her name.

"Miss Wentworth, may I walk with you?" Emmett asked. "It appears that we both have the same idea."

"Yes, of course, Mr. Bentley," she replied. She thought he looked exceptionally dapper in his long, tailored tweed coat complimented by contrasting cream-colored cravat. He, too, was wearing leather gloves and sturdy leather boots. His bowler hat added a touch of sophistication.

Emmett offered his arm. Under a translucent blue sky, Eliza walked with Emmett, the snow crunching underfoot. The warmth of the sun was a great relief engulfing her in a soothing embrace.

Evidence of melting snow was everywhere with puddles of water resulting from the disappearing snow drifts.

Amused with Emmett's attentiveness and witty manner, she smiled and laughed. He then shifted to conversation centered primarily on himself.

"Miss Wentworth, I am an only child. When I was younger, I often traveled with my parents. With our home only twenty miles from London, we spent considerable time there and have been to some of the finest places."

"What are your special interests, Mr. Bentley?" Eliza asked.

"Believe it or not, I like to follow men and women's fashion trends and popular sought-after products. I have a few acquaintances that deal in merchandising and I have given them some of my opinions of what will sell well, and I'm usually correct."

"With your acumen, you could become an importer-exporter," she said, showing surprise. "I understand there is more and more demand for imports."

"I have considered that," Emmett replied. "But when your needs are already met, there is little motivation. I will inherit my parents' large estate, and even now receive a generous sum per annum. I have never been overly concerned about money."

"I understand that many men from privileged backgrounds often choose vocations, much like Thomas has with his business dealings. He seems quite forward-thinking," Eliza mentioned casually.

Emmett grimaced. "Regarding my cousin, I hold him in high esteem, but at times he can be very obstinate. I've tried unsuccessfully to persuade him to invest a bit on the horses. When I suggested it, he was adamant about not wanting to gamble on horse racing, and discouraged me from doing so. As luck would have it, I lost money on a horse that was supposed to be a sure winner. When I asked Thomas for a small loan to carry me through for a week or two, he refused and said I had brought it on myself. I have found that once Thomas has made his mind up about something, particularly concerning money, he rarely budges. Stubborn as a mule!"

Eliza found it most improper that Emmett would speak ill of

Thomas, especially when they were guests in his home. She questioned Emmett's motives. Could he be jealous of his cousin, or still resentful he wasn't given the requested money? She also thought it a bit uncouth, even childish, of Emmett to squander his money on betting on horse races, and couldn't fault Thomas for refusing to save Emmett from a well-earned comeuppance.

"By the way, how are you enjoying being in Amersham?" she continued politely just the same. It wasn't her place to scold him.

"It is tolerable. I much prefer London with its many diversions like markets and shops, the impressive public buildings like Tower Bridge and the many museums," he admitted.

"I like the shops too, as well as the museums, the lovely ornate buildings, and even the gas lights. However, I do not enjoy the London fog. I love living in Amersham. I guess you can say that I find enjoyment in the country as well as in the city. Each has its own merits, as well as its disadvantages."

"That speaks well of you, Miss Wentworth," Emmett said, pausing to squeeze her hand. "I enjoy the country more, especially with you being here." He gave her a charming smile—the kind that had captivated many young women in London, as Eliza recalled.

"That's very generous of you, Mr. Bentley," she replied. A twinge of uneasiness showed on her face. She wasn't immune to Emmett's flattering attention, but couldn't help but think of Thomas.

As they returned to the manor, a large puddle had formed on the pathway. Emmett grasped both Eliza's hands and lifted her over it. Walking side by side, Eliza saw Thomas approaching and felt suddenly self-conscious being on the arm of Emmett.

"Good day, Miss Wentworth, Emmett." Thomas nodded.

"We decided to go for a walk," Emmett said, indicating it was a mutual choice. "Is everything sorted with the heating system?"

"Mr. Harrison found and fixed the issue," Thomas replied. "It should stay warm now. These things happen from time to time, and I like to watch so I can learn for myself. Now, if you'll excuse me, I need to attend to some other matters," he added before walking away briskly.

After spending a delightful afternoon with Thomas the day before, Eliza could only imagine he must think of her as a terrible flirt. On the other hand, she reasoned, as an unattached woman it was perfectly proper to be in the company of another gentleman, even if he was Thomas's cousin.

She decided she might as well just get on with her day and contemplate the many irksome problems of being an unattached woman later.

Before afternoon tea, Eliza and the children went on a treasure hunt that proved wildly successful. Then Eliza took everyone to the sitting room to make Christmas cards and treat cones to be hung on the bedchamber doors.

"Looks like you have been busy at work," Thomas remarked, entering the room and examining the finished projects.

"Papa, look what I made." Pamela proudly held up a Christmas treat cone.

"Very nice, dear."

"We used to do this with Mum," Ned remarked, his voice carrying a hint of nostalgia. His eyes reflected a tinge of sadness. Eliza's heart was touched by the bittersweet memory he shared about his mother.

Eager to preserve the excitement generated by the children, she glanced at Thomas and remarked, "They have done a wonderful job." With a smile, she handed him a card that Ned had designed. "I believe you may have a budding artist in the making."

"I like it very much, son." Ned's face lit up with his father's praise, his pleasure evident in his expression.

"When do you plan on delivering the candy cones?" Thomas asked.

"Tomorrow, Papa, early in the morning. We want it to be a surprise," Ned said with excitement, eagerly looking forward to the delivery.

"Perhaps I can help?" Thomas offered.

"Of course." Eliza smiled, pleased that he wanted to help. "In the morning, before everyone is awake, please bring the children to the landing on the second floor. I'll have everything ready in the library."

"I can do that, Miss Wentworth," he said.

Eliza put her fingers to her lips. "Remember, children, we need to keep this secret, and we will need to be very quiet."

As the children ran off to engage in their next diversion, Eliza and Thomas gathered up the candy cones.

"Miss Wentworth," Thomas began. "About—"

"I hope I'm not interrupting anything," Emmett said as he entered the room. In truth, his smile conveyed that he didn't much care if he was interrupting. "I saw the children just now, and they said they have a surprise for everyone, but wouldn't say what."

"Good for them. I didn't know if they could do it." Thomas looked pleased with the children, though exasperated when he looked at Emmett.

"It's hard to keep track of what's going on around here and I didn't have anything to do, so I came to search for Miss Wentworth," Emmett said, clearly annoyed.

"Emmett, if you're bored you're welcome to go riding, get a card game going, play Match Darts, or get a book from the library," Thomas suggested matter-of-factly.

Eliza suppressed a smile. "I think I had better go dress for dinner," she said, excusing herself from the room. Emmett also left, muttering to himself.

Despite the obvious tension between Thomas and Emmett, dinner went smoothly, with pleasant conversation. Toward the end, Thomas looked out at the sky. "It's such a clear night, those who like to do some star gazing come to the observatory." Only Eliza, Emmett and Miss Saunders chose to go.

While Thomas was adjusting the telescope, Emmett escorted Eliza and Jane into the room, which glowed with soft, warm light from gas lights. Garlands and a few wreaths adorned the walls, accented by pots of vibrant red poinsettias. Near the fireplace sat a decorated Christmas tree, adding a perfect touch to a most festive setting. Eliza,

Jane Saunders, and Emmett each sat on one of the four chairs arranged closely around a central table that held a few star maps and other charts. The seating arrangement created an intimate space.

Eliza gazed through one of the three large windows, marveling at the twinkling stars against the velvety night sky. "It's magnificent, Lord Bentley. Even without a telescope."

"My great-grandfather had a great love of astronomy and had the room carefully designed. That door at the end of the room leads to a porch where the telescope may be moved outside. Would you care to look, Miss Wentworth?" Thomas asked.

She stepped up and looked through the lens. "I can see the Milky Way and the North Star. They look so vibrant up close," Eliza remarked. "I've never seen anything quite like it."

Emmett and Jane Saunders also each took a turn. Emmett had looked through the telescope before, and quickly relinquished it to Miss Saunders, taking a seat next to Eliza.

Chatting with Emmett, Eliza tried to concentrate on what he was saying, but her thoughts were far away, wondering why she felt a shade of jealousy and insecurity as Thomas and Jane stood laughing and talking together.

Worse yet, when they decided to sit down, Thomas did not take the chair located next to Eliza, but instead guided Jane to the chair, and sat down beside her. This all was very cozy, but Eliza felt as if she was mistakenly connected with Emmett, while Thomas was engaging with Jane. It was most disconcerting.

Jane talked about her father's voyages, explaining how he used the stars, charts, and a compass to navigate. He would often come home with adventuresome tales as well as ghost stories, including the famous legend of "The Flying Dutchman." Thomas and Emmett listened intently as she spun the tale. Eliza tried, but her thoughts were too fixated on Thomas and Jane.

Afterward, Thomas suggested they call it a night and offered his arm to Jane. Her evident pleasure at the gesture was unmistakable. That was the gentlemanly thing to do, Eliza tried to convince herself as she took Emmett's arm.

As Eliza prepared for bed, Daisy brushed her hair, and Eliza reflected on her day. Did she really have the attention of two men, or were their interests divided between her and Jane Saunders? The situation was unsettling, leaving her to question the intentions of both and feeling confused. After these past years of not encouraging any attachments, her mother would likely see this as a favorable dilemma. But Eliza felt uneasy, trying to sort out her own feelings and navigate the situation.

THE GLASSHOUSE

*B*efore the rooster crowed, or the sun had made its appearance, Thomas, children in tow, knocked on Eliza's bedchamber door. She appeared at the door, looking as appealing as a strawberry ice on a warm summer day. Her silk dress with small cream and pink stripes and tiny embossed lavender flowers seemed to flow as she walked. Thomas couldn't take his eyes off her.

"Good morning, Miss Wentworth. You look especially lovely this morning."

Before she could respond, Ned began tugging on his father's arm. "Papa, can we get the candy cones now?" he whispered.

"Of course, son. They are in the library," he said, barely able to chase thoughts of Eliza away.

Gathering up the paper cones, they quietly hung one on each bedchamber door. There were lots of giggles and loud "shushing" noises as they walked through the hall.

Daniel, who never missed a trick, opened his door. "How did this get here? Who could have left it?" Abigail couldn't contain her excitement for more than a minute and rushed forward.

"We did, Papa!" He picked her up, kissing her on the check. "It's the best surprise ever. Thank you, Abigail."

The children burst into giggles as they watched each door open. Emmett feigned a surprised face and gave each one a peppermint stick. In their exuberance, the children ran and hugged Thomas, knocking him to the ground. He was soon smothered by their rowdy hugs and laughter that echoed through the hall. Looking up, he saw Eliza laughing, enjoying every moment of this playful chaos. This was a side of him few people ever saw, but he was glad Eliza was one of them.

"GLASSHOUSE! LORD BENTLEY HAS A GLASSHOUSE?" Eliza exclaimed.

She'd just been looking for fresh mint for her tea when she ran into Mrs. Adams and queried her about where she might find some.

"Oh yes, miss. It is not as large and grand as some, but it is one of Lord Bentley's favorite places," Mrs. Adams explained with a warm smile. "He helps the Head Gardener, Bert, grow all kinds of plants and flowers. As they don't get too much heat or cold, a number of flowers and fruits are available year round. Bert carefully watches over each plant, and is very protective of his little treasures."

"Where is the glasshouse? I would love to see it," Eliza said.

"It's adjacent to the back of the house. You will want your wellies. There's puddles out there!" Mrs. Adams called after her.

Soon, Eliza was maneuvering between the pools of water, grateful Mrs. Adams had suggested wearing wellies. The glasshouse was something to behold. Mrs. Adams had been modest when describing it. There were large glass windows framed with ornate wood and metal. The double doors had a combination of glass and wooden louvers, which she surmised were for ventilation when needed.

Once inside, the aroma of flowers and herbs permeated the air. As Eliza walked on the stone floor, she saw wicker furniture placed throughout the room, surrounded by plants and flowers. Lovely hanging baskets with a plethora of flowers and greenery, visible throughout the glasshouse, created a sense of beauty and tranquility.

Moving toward the wood-burning stove, she noted flowers in pots that were the same variety as those displayed in the manor.

But most intriguing was a strawberry plant in bloom. "Strawberries, and in winter! What a delight!" she exclaimed out loud, unable to resist eating two or three. Just then, the door opened.

"I see you are stealing my strawberries," Thomas chided as he approached her. Eliza stood, startled by his sudden appearance and then breathed a sigh of relief.

"Forgive me, Miss Wentworth, for taking you by surprise. Mrs. Adams said you were here."

"I will forgive you, if you forgive me for eating your delicious strawberries."

"Fair enough. There are still seven remaining."

"You count them?" she asked curiously.

"I do, daily," Thomas replied. "I like to work alongside Bert, who is very precise with the under-gardeners and keeps everything carefully tended to."

"Let me show you some of my favorite flowers," Thomas continued, pointing with enthusiasm. "Here are azaleas, and the purple ones are rhododendrons."

Eliza moved closer to a yellow plant. "This must be a hyacinth. I can smell its sweet fragrance. My mother grows those in the spring."

"My prized flowers are the orchids." Thomas gestured to a collection of orchids in deep purples and pink to elegant white.

"Aren't they hard to grow?" Eliza asked, intrigued.

Thomas nodded. "They can be. Orchids need a delicate balance of sunlight and moisture to thrive."

Carefully examining a fern, Eliza suddenly started frantically screaming.

"Miss Wentworth, what is it?" Thomas asked urgently.

Gulping, she pulled back, continuing to scream. "There's a hideous spider on that plant!"

LIFTING her up and perching her on a small, nearby bench, Thomas grabbed a nearby trowel. He quickly reached down, caught the spider, and flung it out of the glasshouse door. Eliza's screams subsided, but she stood trembling.

Thomas gently lifted her from her perch, and held onto her until she was calm. Although they had shared a similar moment before, the warmth of her resting against him, and the faint whiff of lilac in her hair stirred feelings he thought were gone. It brought back memories of the night of the storm when she hugged him upon his return from rescuing the Suttons. Her presence brought with it emotions he hadn't fully acknowledged.

Once the crisis was over, and Eliza had calmed, they continued through the glasshouse. As they passed the gardenias, Thomas reached out, picked a bloom, and handed it to her. "Miss Wentworth," he said with a warm smile, "please put this by your bedside. Gardenias bring sweet thoughts."

"Why thank you," she replied. "I consider this a very special gift."

She took the arm he offered, and they strolled out of the glasshouse, making their way back to the manor, where preparations for lunch were already underway. The aroma of freshly-baked bread filled the air, mingling with the hum of pleasant conversation.

THOMAS FOUND himself alone with Daniel in the afternoon and couldn't resist sharing the incident from the glasshouse earlier. With a chuckle he said, "For such a brave woman when dealing with a crisis, I had no idea a spider could be so menacing. I'll never understand women!"

Daniel grinned and replied, "I find it best not to try."

"However," Thomas added, "I can't feel too sorry about the appearance of the spider when the results were so enjoyable. These past few days spent with Miss Wentworth have caused me to think about the pleasure of having a woman like her in my life, and how easily we've rekindled our friendship."

"Is it just friendship, though?" Daniel asked.

Thomas considered. "It could develop into something more. I want to use this time to understand her desires. Despite her beauty and charm, she has remained unmarried for several years and seems quite content at Wentworth Manor."

Daniel responded, "However, there are few opportunities for marriage for someone of her stature in Amersham."

Thomas sighed, "Every time I try to spend time with her, Emmett steps in. I thought Emmett might be interested in Miss Saunders, given their ages. She is certainly a lovely young lady."

"Miss Saunders seems conflicted," Daniel stated. "Though, her flirting has been directed to you."

Thomas agreed, "I find that flattering, but it feels more like the affection of a younger sister. She will understand more when she has her first season and mixes with the ton."

"Well, with your eyes perhaps set on the charming Miss Wentworth, it is a wonder you're wasting time talking to me," Daniel grinned.

"True. I shall see you later, Daniel."

Thomas quickly sought out Eliza, finding her in the library reading her detective novel.

"Miss Wentworth," Thomas said, already armed with an excuse. "I need to deliver a Christmas box to the Hopwood family this afternoon, as they're leaving town in a few days. Would you like to join me? Daisy will be with us as chaperone, of course."

"I would love to," Eliza replied. "How soon are you leaving?"

"I'd like to go now, whenever you are ready, if that isn't rushing you too much."

"Not at all," Eliza said. "I'll get my coat and fetch Daisy." Eliza rose from her seat. "We'll come down to the entryway, if that suits you."

"Excellent," Thomas replied with pleasure. "I'll have the coach brought around."

SOON THEY WERE RIDING in the coach, jolted as it bumped along, hitting ruts here and there. Daisy, sitting across from Eliza and Thomas, occupied herself knitting. The rhythmic sway of the coach caused Eliza and Thomas's shoulders to touch occasionally. It brought a touch of color to Eliza's cheeks.

As Eliza peered out the window, her gaze was drawn to a small grove of trees nearby.

"Lord Bentley," she exclaimed, pointing to the grove, "I saw a building over there, and there was a sign over the door that read 'schoolhouse.' You have a schoolhouse?"

Thomas leaned over to look out the window. His closeness sent shivers down her spine.

"It's a modest place but it serves its purpose. I had a coach house converted into a schoolhouse. Sometimes the tenants gather there for communal eating, or occasional dances."

"Who teaches the children?" Eliza asked.

"Vicar Pike and his daughter, Ashley, come two times a week. The children are taught from the Bible as well as from primers. Each student has their own slate and chalk."

"I think that is just marvelous," she said with genuine delight. "Your tenants are very fortunate. You care about them far much more than other landowners I have met."

"Are you familiar with other properties?" Thomas asked.

"I am. I've seen a number of them on medical visits with Dr. Dyer," she explained.

"Miss Wentworth, do you mind if I call you by your Christian name?"

"Not at all. If that is agreeable to you, I'll do the same," she said, pleased that he would make that request.

"Now that we have that settled, Eliza, you amaze me. You certainly haven't kept yourself at home, with limited knowledge about what is going on around you."

"I just can't do that. I've tried to immerse myself in stitchery, reading, gardening, and social visits, but there has to be more to life than that. That's why I started learning medicine and helping Dr. Dyer. I want to do something meaningful that makes a difference until I have a family of my own."

Thomas, curious, asked, "What about after you are married? Or is that too personal?"

"No, I'm happy to answer that question. I've thought about it a great deal. I think marriage and having children should be a woman's first priority. It certainly is mine. Not all women are gifted in the arts of homemaking, and that is why I've learned medical skills. Besides, Dr. Dyer has told me he thinks any skills I learn now will only benefit my future family."

"A very wise man," Thomas stated.

"I was once in love with the prospect of marriage," Eliza said with a touch of regret in her voice. "Sadly, the young man was a victim of his family's financial ruin, and my father brought me back to Amersham in the middle of my second season. I know it was for my own benefit, but it was heartbreaking, and I doubted my own judgment in such matters. Since then, I have remained guarded about forming attachments. My father asked me not to discuss it with anyone."

"Eliza, what you've just shared is certainly personal and delicate. Going through such an experience as a young woman must have been very trying, and I understand how it must have affected your feelings and thoughts. However, rising above it and developing your skills to serve others is commendable," he responded, his tone warm and sincere. "I find your company to be very pleasant." He then gently kissed her fingers, still gloved in leather.

Daisy cleared her throat, but Eliza still said to him in a soft tone, "Thomas, being with you makes me feel secure, as though you genuinely have my best interests at heart. That is very reassuring to me and makes me feel valued."

Thomas replied, "You are important to me, Eliza. You truly are."

This made Eliza blush, her feelings all aflutter. "Thank you," she said.

They descended into a comfortable silence as they reached the Hopwood residence. Thomas, carrying a large box, and Eliza entered the cottage first, followed by Daisy.

Mr. Hopwood immediately took the box, setting it on a nearby table where a basket of pinecones and a red candle had been placed. His calloused hands spoke of the hard work he did. A foot taller than his petite wife, they both greeted their esteemed visitors in a proper, but friendly, way.

"We're honored to have you here, Lord Bentley and Miss Wentworth and Miss Daisy," Mr. Hopwood said. "We're mighty grateful for your visit and the box of food."

"It is a pleasure. You are good tenants, and we've come to wish you a Happy Christmas," Thomas replied.

Eliza surveyed the room that served as a space for dining and all other activities. Most noticeable were the paper snowflakes and stars that decorated the windows where muslin curtains hung. The modest dwelling had two bedrooms, a loft overhead and a small kitchen. A braided rug created a sense of coziness and warmth. Next to the stone fireplace was wood, neatly stacked. A young boy lay on a makeshift cot near the hearth.

Thomas asked that Eliza and Daisy be introduced to the family.

"I'd be delighted," Mrs. Hopwood said proudly. "Our five children are our gems." Eliza marveled at how a large family could fit so compactly in such a small space—or how they could even function.

"These are our daughters, Lindsay and Emilee," Mrs. Hopwood said as two attractive young girls, who looked very much like their mother, emerged from the kitchen. With sweet smiles, the girls served their guests pan gingerbread and cups of tea.

"Lord Bentley, I'm right pleased to say that my girls are learning to cook on the stovetop you had put in," Mrs. Hopwood expressed gratefully.

"I'm pleased you like it," Thomas replied, tasting the gingerbread. "I feel it is good to make progress and improve things whenever you can."

Just then, a young boy lying on a makeshift cot near the fireplace, began having a coughing fit. Mrs. Hopwood moved to his side, offering him sips of water. "This here is our youngest son, Jonah," she said, her voice full of concern. "He would be out feeding the chickens and gathering eggs, but he has been miserable for the last few days."

"Before we leave, if you will allow her," Thomas said. "Miss Wentworth has medical experience and has worked with our local doctor, Dr. Dyer, and can offer her assistance." He glanced at Eliza to confirm her willingness. She nodded in approval.

"We would be beholden to you," Mrs. Hopwood said, looking weary.

Mr. Hopwood continued to introduce their two other sons. "Gary, our oldest, reads right well, thanks to your school, Lord Bentley. We all love to hear him read from the books he brings home. This is Josh, our middle son. He'd rather be outdoors, collecting bugs and taking care of our animals."

"I once nursed a wounded rabbit back to health. " Josh spoke up proudly. "I also make sure to leave seeds and nuts for the squirrels during the winter."

"Josh, that is a very fine thing to do," Thomas said with approval. "Maybe one day when you're older, you can help animals even more."

Eliza marveled at the ease Thomas spoke with the Hopwoods. He treated them with respect, with no condescending attitude unlike those, such as Emmett, who were acutely aware of rank and prominence.

Daisy took a seat next to the Hopwoods' daughters and engaged them in conversation, offering them some of the treats she had brought along. She beckoned to the two boys to come over, and shared treats with them as well. Her presence helped the Hopwood children feel at ease.

When there was a lull in the conversation Eliza said, "Mrs. Hopwood, if I might suggest mint tea with honey and lemon will help ease your son's coughing. I have found that rubbing menthol on the chest, as well as breathing vapors from a very warm cloth, helps break up the congestion."

"Thank you kindly, Miss Wentworth, but we have none of them things," Mrs. Hopwood responded sadly.

"When we return, I will have them brought to you," Thomas interjected, "along with one of my son's favorite books, *The Swiss Family Robinson*. Gary can read it to the family. It's a great adventure tale."

"Also, Mrs. Hopwood, if Jonah doesn't start to improve immediately, please send word, and I'll send for Dr. Dyer. Don't worry about the cost. I will see to it," Thomas assured her.

"Thank you, Lord Bentley. We're so grateful for your visit today, and you as well, Miss Wentworth. I'll follow your instructions for Jonah. And the treats that Daisy shared have delighted the children." Tears welled up in Mrs. Hopwood's eyes as they left to board the coach.

The ride back to the manor was a comfortable one. "It's satisfying to see that a family can be happy in any circumstances," Eliza said. "You have made life better for them, Thomas, with the care you give to them. Thank you for letting me come with you today."

"You being there made the visit much easier. Mrs. Hopwood barely said anything when I was there last year. I know she felt more comfortable having a woman there as well. Your medical suggestion was done so kindly. She was able to speak honestly, so we could help her. Well done, my dear."

My dear! Eliza was elated like she had just found a long-lost treasure.

When they returned to the manor, Eliza retreated to her room and settled into the cozy chaise, wrapped in a satin throw while reading her book. As she took a break, she noticed shadows dancing about on the wall. *Oh, no. I'm going to be late for dinner!* She quickly closed the book.

Fortunately, she had prepared ahead and was dressed in a light green dress with a white insert at the neckline. The small pleats at her skirt's hem were swaying with each step she took as she sheepishly entered the dining room.

"Fashionably late," Thomas said quietly as she took her seat. She blushed with awareness that dinner had not yet been served. Her disregard for promptness had become normal—almost expected of her. It was a complete contrast to Thomas's punctuality. She recommitted herself for, who knows how many times, to be on time.

"How was your visit to the Hopwoods?" Lily inquired.

"Yes, how was your visit with the lower classes, Thomas?" Emmett asked with a hint of disdain.

A brief silence fell over the table before Thomas responded, "Very satisfactory. It's rewarding for me to see how my tenants have benefited from having their own school and improvements to their cottages." He turned to Eliza. "What did you think, Miss Wentworth?"

Eliza looked momentarily flustered. "I never realized what was involved in overseeing a vast property like Bentley Manor and the surrounding estate. Caring for the needs of tenants is a great responsibility," Eliza said thoughtfully. "Mr. and Mrs. Hopwood and their children were most congenial and treated us with respect. It was a new experience for me, but one that I truly value."

Admiral Saunders added, "I've known landowners who do the bare minimum for their tenants. It's a sad situation—it keeps the children from progressing and limits their opportunities. I've known of boys as young as twelve or thirteen who have joined the merchant navy that carry goods between countries, or fishing boats. Young girls must go into homes doing domestic service as young as ten or eleven."

Emmett paused, clearly taken aback by the conversation. "I have to admit," he said slowly, choosing his words carefully, "I wasn't aware of the extent of the difficulties faced by the tenants. I suppose it's easy to overlook these realities when one's experiences have been of a different nature."

Emmett then lifted his glass of wine. "To you, Thomas," he said, his tone more sincere than usual. The others at the table followed suit, raising their glasses in agreement. The clinking of glass filled the room, acknowledging Thomas's efforts. Eliza caught Thomas's eye and smiled, enjoying the well-earned praise that Thomas deserved.

As they toasted Thomas, he shifted uncomfortably in his chair, a modest smile tugging at his lips. "Well, thank you everyone, I didn't expect that." Then with a nod, he signaled Kingsley to have dessert served.

At the completion of dinner, Lily announced that a pantomime of

"Goldilocks and the Three Bears" would be the night's entertainment. The drawing room had been set up like a theater with two rows of chairs. Daniel played the part of Baby Bear. Abigail was Mama Bear. Ned, Papa Bear, and Pamela made a perfect Goldilocks. At the conclusion, everyone joined in singing "For He's a Jolly Good Fellow."

The satisfaction that Thomas felt seeing his children perform was apparent, and his compliments were rewarded with radiant, joyous smiles from Ned and Pamela. With an arm around each of them, he promised to come and say goodnight.

"Would you care to come with me, Eliza?" Thomas asked.

"I don't want to intrude."

"I believe Ned and Pamela would like having you there." Both children nodded.

Eliza was not proof against such a sweet request and helped to escort the children up the stairs. Entering the nursery, Eliza observed that Ned and Pamela each had their own special place. Pictures of horses and ships decorated the walls by Ned's bed. Books and toys were neatly arranged on shelves.

"I like your room very much," Eliza said. "What is your favorite toy?"

He eagerly pointed to a zoetrope reel. When he turned it on, it created the illusion of animated festive Christmas scenes by spinning drawings inside a cylinder. "Mum and Papa gave it to me."

"He received it on his third birthday," Thomas said. He began to reminisce about that very happy day filled with presents and cake. It was the last one Julia celebrated with her family.

Although she had been invited to nursery, she felt like an outsider peeking through a window as Thomas and Ned reminisced about his third birthday. Thomas then hugged his son, bidding him goodnight. Eliza was pleased when Ned gave her a slight wave and a smile, making her feel a little more comfortable.

Pamela's nook was decorated in pale pink. Several dolls in a small doll carriage sat near a doll house filled with miniature furniture that Thomas mentioned Julia had selected.

When Thomas tenderly tucked Pamela into bed, Eliza remained

silent. Standing near Pamela's bedside, Eliza had a sense of unease again. Julia should be here, doing this.

Unexpectedly Pamela reached up and put her arms around her. With Pamela's hug, her apprehension melted away, and she saw only the pure love of a child that warmed her soul.

"Sweet dreams," was all Eliza could say, choking back tears.

As they left the nursery, Eliza thought about Thomas, faced with raising children alone. Evidence of Julia's devotion surrounded them. Eliza couldn't imagine life without her own mother. How could anyone take a mother's place?

Seeing Julia's portrait at the top of the stairs brought on more tears. "I'm so sorry," Eliza began as Thomas handed her a handkerchief. "Tonight was so touching—the way you treat your children with such loving care. It's evident how much you shoulder."

Thomas reached out and took her hand. "I grapple with that, and try to do my best. My desire is to provide as happy and secure a childhood for Ned and Pamela as possible."

"You are doing wonderfully. They are a real part of your life, Thomas, and you are there for them. They are lovely children and so delightful to be with," Eliza said.

"I thought about Julia tonight, and our loss. Having her as my wife and their mother—it's something a father can't replace, no matter how he tries. There are things like a mother's nurturing that a father cannot do in the same way. I've been thinking about their future, and about them growing up without a mother to turn to. Of course, they have caring grandmothers and lovely aunts, but it's not the same." Thomas looked as if he wanted to say more, but stopped.

Eliza didn't press him further. They had shared quite a few confidences that day. Walking her to her bedchamber door, Thomas lightly brushed her cheek with his fingers. "Good night, Eliza. Thank you for listening and being with me today."

She looked up and smiled, feeling a peaceful contentment. "Good night, Thomas."

They stood there for a few moments looking at each other. Things had changed between them.

THE BLUE DANUBE WALTZ

*T*he manor was bustling with activity. Preparations were underway for the Christmas Ball to be held that evening. Greenery had been added over all the doorways and was wrapped around the stairway with shimmering gold bows tied every few feet. Excitement filled the air as housemaids and footmen scurried with silver trays and elegant white tablecloths in hand. Additional staff, hired for the occasion, began arriving and helping to prepare the food. Elaborate vases of flowers and silver candelabras were carefully arranged throughout the great room.

Kingsley, directing the activities with the precision of a seasoned police officer navigating a busy London street, orchestrated the bustling scene. Thomas, lending a helping hand, ensured every detail met the standard of elegance befitting the occasion.

The children were wild with excitement, and pleaded to stay up and watch the guests arrive. "I want to see the pretty dresses. Can I, Papa? Can I?" Pamela pleaded.

Scratching his head, Thomas said, "You're only four, and are already interested in fashion." He sighed. "Yes, you may. You children can watch from the top of the stairway, but you must promise when the nanny comes to take you to bed you won't fuss."

"We promise," Ned and Pamela said in unison.

Thomas smiled affectionately and tousled his son's hair. "You are a good boy, Ned. And Pamela, you are my little princess."

As he had no specific plans for the day, Thomas left his guests to choose whatever they wished to do. Daniel and Lily prepared to take the children sledding on a nearby hill, and invited Eliza to join them. To be outdoors was a treat for Eliza, as well as an opportunity to be with Pamela and Ned.

Daniel carefully selected gentle slopes for Pamela and Abigail. He and Ned went down more challenging ones. Eliza enjoyed a ride or two herself. She had dressed in her new divided skirt, navy winter coat, and leather boots, hoping for a chance to ride. She remembered the fun she had as a child—gliding down the hills, the wind in her hair and the sheer delight of it all. As memories of her childhood lingered in her mind, she was suddenly part of a friendly snowball fight—girls against boys. Eliza's coat was soon dotted with snow that had the appearance of large, white polka dots.

They returned shortly after the snowball fight. Eliza headed upstairs to shed her winter gear. The painting of Julia caught her eye. Would she be betraying a friend by falling in love with her husband? The question lingered in her mind like a delicate whisper. How could she be drawn to Thomas in such a short time? Her feelings for him were blossoming like one of his roses.

"She was beautiful, wasn't she? And such a devoted wife." Emmett unexpectedly was beside her.

"She was." Eliza nodded in agreement.

"She must have left an indelible mark on Thomas's heart. It would be difficult for anyone else to take her place. I don't believe he has seriously pursued any other woman."

"Have you been around Lord Bentley enough to know that?" she questioned.

"Well, it's been three years since Julia's passing, and I'm not aware of Thomas escorting any woman to a family gathering or any other event I've attended. Our Grandmother Bentley has often expressed she wished he could find someone new, but she wonders if that will ever happen."

Eliza questioned Emmett's motives for his remarks. Was he endeavoring to caution her about her growing admiration for his cousin, or was it because of his own self-interest?

Feeling the need to gather her thoughts, Eliza politely excused herself and went to her room. She resolved to set aside uncertainty, and enjoy the evening. While immersed in her book, she heard the commotion downstairs, and her curiosity overcame her.

As she descended the staircase, Eliza admired the lush evergreen garland on the banister, adorned with velvet bows, ornaments, and silver and gold accents. A grand arch, decorated similarly, framed the entrance to the Great Room. As she entered, she felt like she was coming into the enchanting world of Christmas.

"What do you think, Eliza?" Thomas asked as he surveyed the room.

"It is magnificent, and nearly brings me to tears," Eliza said, almost in a whisper. He squeezed her and gave an appreciative smile.

"Come walk with me," he said. Together they strolled through the room.

"I love the Nativity tapestry and the woodland scenes you've added, Thomas," she said, noticing the addition of sofas and padded chairs. Eliza wondered if Thomas had helped plan previous parties held here. He did not seem to be a novice.

They strolled past long tables covered in white linen with silver candelabras, topiary trees, and sprays of beautiful flowers. Soon the tables would hold silver trays of cakes, biscuits, bonbons, meats, and sandwiches. Next to the elegant cut-glass punch bowls were piles of roasted nuts.

"Most of the crystal dishes, serving trays, and many of the decorations are remnants of the lavish parties that my grandparents hosted. Especially grand was their annual Christmas party. I want to revive that tradition," Thomas said.

Locking his eyes with hers, he asked, "May I escort you to the ball tonight?" She remembered Emmett's comment about Thomas not having escorted a woman to a social event in three years. Although she had hoped he would ask her, she was pleasantly surprised when he did.

"I would be honored," she replied, "but after you have welcomed your guests. This is your evening, and I don't want to take away from that in any way." She also wanted to avoid having people speculate about her and Thomas's relationship. As they continued talking, she felt a flutter of excitement, thinking of the coming evening.

THAT AFTERNOON, she soaked in a leisurely warm bath, the scent of rose water enveloping her. Having hot water running directly into the home was such a delightful luxury.

Daisy finally persuaded her to leave the bath, then helped her get ready. She styled her hair in a modern-looking updo with several curls framing her face. Eliza's choice of cranberry silk had been right and emphasized her fair skin and chestnut hair. The off-the-shoulder bodice trimmed with delicate beige lace fit her perfectly. As she walked, her skirt draped and flowed along the floor at just the right length for dancing. The perfect touch was her mother's clear crystal necklace and earrings.

As she viewed her ensemble in the oval mirror, she was pleased with her reflection, and felt confident tonight would be enchanting— not just because of the gown, but because she would be wearing it with Thomas as her escort.

"Ah, Miss Eliza, you're lookin' fair lovely, you are," Daisy beamed.

Eliza smiled and gave Daisy a hug. Pulling on her long white gloves, she spun around and opened the door, surprised to see Kingsley.

"Lord Bentley is in the foyer greeting the last of his guests and would like you to join him." She followed him out into the hall and stood at the top of the staircase.

Standing on the landing in her elegant gown, Eliza saw Thomas looking up at her with an admiring gaze. Once she descended, he took her hand and said, "You look beautiful, Eliza. Exquisite."

Thomas in his black tailcoat formal wear, white shirt and white bowtie looked strikingly handsome. "Thank you, Thomas, you look very distinguished yourself." Being on the arm of Thomas felt like something she read about in one of her novels, but this was happening to her. She felt she was on the arm of the most desirable man in the room.

Eliza was introduced to Thomas's neighbors, many of whom she already knew. Emmett declared she looked divine and requested two dances. She blushed as she handed him her dance card. Emmett's persistence in gaining her attention was evident, while her feelings for Thomas became increasingly clear. Her doubts were fading away.

To have local musicians, especially at this time of year, was a great treat. There was an ensemble of violists, a harpist, a flute player, and a cellist. Eliza remained close to Thomas speaking to several guests, and complemented Jane Saunders on her lovely cream-colored gown. Jane looked disappointed when she saw Eliza on Thomas's arm, but quickly recovered and resumed her gracious smile.

Thomas claimed Eliza for the first dance. After they took their place on the floor, several other couples, both married and unmarried, joined them. The first dance was a quadrille. As Thomas and Eliza bowed, and joined hands, a subtle thrill of excitement and sense of connection quietly flowed between them, making this moment different from an ordinary hand-holding encounter. Eliza moved easily by his side. Dancing with him was a treat.

Emmett claimed Eliza for the next dance, moving with expert grace as they circled near Thomas and Jane. Thomas kept his focus strictly on Jane, a pleasant look on his face as if he were not aware of Emmett's presence at all. With each step, he purposefully moved in the opposite direction. Seeing Jane and Thomas together, some of Eliza's old doubts began to surface. After all, he had asked to escort her to the dance. But did he have to look like he was enjoying dancing with Miss Saunders that much?

Once the dance ended, Emmett escorted Eliza to her seat, placing her next to Admiral and Mrs. Saunders. "My compliments, Mr. Bentley. You and Miss Wentworth dance very well together," Admiral Saunders said. Emmett responded with a nod and a proud smile, his expression remaining until Thomas joined them.

"Lord Bentley, the ball is exceptional. Such a fine evening, especially at this joyous time of year. We are having a New Year's Eve Gala and certainly want you all to come. Invitations are forthcoming," Mrs. Saunders said with pleasure. Her fancy headdress with a lavender feather atop complemented her beaded lavender gown.

"Thank you, Mrs. Saunders. Surrounded by friends like you and your family, I feel at home again," Thomas replied.

Thomas claimed Eliza for the next dance. As they walked away, Emmett's expression remained neutral, only his eyes revealing his simmering frustration. "The Blue Danube" was being played, and was one of her favorites. Thomas and Eliza glided across the floor with elegant steps and turns, moving with perfect harmony with the gentle rhythm of the waltz. At the conclusion of the music, they stood looking into each other's eyes, unspoken emotions surfacing. Thomas's hand remained on the small of her back, his free hand intertwined with hers. The moment was gone when Emmett walked up to them.

"Would you care to join Miss Saunders and I for some refreshments?" Emmett asked, rather abruptly. The enchanting moment shared by Thomas and Eliza flitted away like a darting hummingbird. Thomas took Eliza's arm and led her to a chair beside Jane Saunders. Eliza smiled and said, "A cup of punch would be lovely."

The two men walked off without exchanging a word. Thomas returned with two delicate crystal cups full of liquid. However, a sudden jolt against his arm, caused by a footman carrying a large tray, resulted in Thomas's cup spilling ruby-red liquid, cascading down the bodice of Eliza's gown. Mortified, the footman stammered out an apology.

"It was just an accident," Thomas said calmly, signaling to Kingsley, who had just witnessed the mishap. The young man was excused to the kitchen where he could do no further damage.

Eliza had taken great care in choosing her gown for this special occasion, and now it was stained with punch. Her emotions were a mix of disappointment, as well as a desire to maintain the happiness she felt. Unsure of what to do, she stood for a moment. Thomas, however, stepped forward to handle the situation.

"Come with me," he said, taking her hand and ushering her into the kitchen.

Looking up from a tray of food, Mrs. Adams spied the stains of Eliza's gown. "Oh, my! Miss Wentworth, please sit here and I'll fetch a cloth."

"I am so sorry this happened. I hope it won't ruin your evening. This is the footman's first time serving," Thomas said.

In that moment of vulnerability, a wave of empathy washed over her. She thought of those who wouldn't have a sip of punch or even a simple meal tonight. She considered her own privileged life and the gratitude she should have.

"There are more important things to fret about than a stained dress," she began. "I hope you will give the footman another chance. I'm sure our dressmaker can take care of it. She is skilled at such things."

Thomas responded with gratitude. "Thank you, Eliza. I'm touched by your kindness." Then Mrs. Adams came over, holding a cloth and handing it to Eliza. "Here, dear," she said, "you can sponge up some of the liquid with this. It should help lessen the stain. You look lovely tonight. Go enjoy the rest of the dance."

They re-entered the room. As master of the house, Thomas was pleased to note that during the evening, all single young ladies had been asked to dance. He ensured that no young lady was left unattended. Thomas and Eliza both danced the remaining dances with a variety of partners. At the end of the ball, Eliza stood nearby while Thomas bade farewell to his guests.

"Thank you, Lord Bentley, for a delightful evening. I wish you and your children a very Merry Christmas," one of the gentlemen said before he and his wife turned to leave.

"And the same to you, sir," Thomas replied. Much to her delight,

Thomas kept Eliza beside him. She found herself less concerned about the opinions of others. The pleasantness of being by his side, feeling his hand holding hers, offered a sense of contentment and belonging.

After the guests had gone, the Great Room was being returned to its normal order with maids and footmen extinguishing candles and removing food, empty dishes, and plates. Tables were in the process of being taken out, along with the linens.

As Thomas and Eliza made their way up the staircase, Eliza was full of compliments. "The Christmas Ball was so lovely. You must feel great satisfaction knowing how successful the evening was."

"Yes, I do feel very content. I had my concerns, but everything went smoothly, other than the unfortunate spill on your gown," Thomas admitted.

"I've forgotten about it already. Don't give it a minute's thought," Eliza assured him. When they reached her bedchamber door, Thomas took both of her hands in his.

"Eliza, being with you tonight has been delightful. I hope the future will continue to be the same, and perhaps lead to something more. May I continue to call upon you?" Thomas asked.

"Yes, I would like that," she replied, her heart dancing with a sweet flutter of excitement. With a smile as bright as a moonbeam, she felt a gentle warmth spreading through her as he lifted her gloved hand and tenderly kissed it. As he walked away, she lingered at the doorway, fully immersing herself in the moment and savoring the happiness she felt.

Her words tumbled out as she told Daisy all about the grandeur of the evening—the decor, the dancing, the delightful food, and even the spilled punch. "The most enchanting part was dancing with Lord Bentley, " she said dreamily as she twirled in a circle. Then she began removing her jewelry.

Eliza tugged on her earlobe, finding it bare. "Oh, I must have lost an earring. It can't be far. Daisy, please lay out my nightclothes," she said as she left the room.

Entering the corridor, she began looking down the hallway. As she moved along, she heard shouting coming from the study. What could that all be about this time of night?

INADVERTENT ENLIGHTENMENT

hrough the open door, Eliza heard Emmett shouting irately, pounding on the desk. "You've managed to keep Miss Wentworth for yourself, Thomas!" She put her hand to her mouth, registering her shock at hearing Thomas and Emmett arguing.

"Emmett, that's not true," she heard Thomas respond calmly. "I have not knowingly tried to keep her from being with anyone. You have accompanied her on several occasions."

"But now I am to accompany the Saunders family home!" Emmett continued to speak in a very harsh voice.

"Miss Saunders, concerned about the health of her father, requested that you go with them. If that did not meet with your approval, Daniel had offered to go. I was willing to give a suitable excuse for you that would not offend her." Thomas's voice remained even.

"Of course, I said I would go," Emmett continued in a slightly more subdued tone. "But what about Miss Wentworth? What are your intentions towards her? It is evident you are in pursuit of her. Thomas, just because of your title, you think you can have whatever you want."

"That's absurd. I have never used my title to influence any woman," he countered. Lashing out again, Emmett said, "Evidently, you've forgotten the vow you made after Julia's death. I clearly remember you saying that losing her had been so devastating that you would never marry again. The pain of losing another wife was not worth the risk. Those were your exact words. Were they not?"

Thomas hesitated for a moment. "Yes, I did vow not to marry again." He breathed a sigh of frustration. "Blast it, Emmett, I do not wish to discuss my personal life with you. Frankly, it is none of your business," Thomas said firmly.

Thomas's irritation was palpable. Hearing these words, tears began to well in Eliza's eyes. She wanted to rush in and confront both men, but as she was the interloper—that would be inexcusable. But it did cause her to wonder. Was Thomas's asking to continue seeing her just a result of the romantic ambiance of the ball? Her doubts, like an uncontrollable wave, crashed over her as she hurried back to her room where she began sobbing.

Daisy, jumping up with a start, immediately cradled Eliza in her arms. Through her sobs, Eliza told Daisy what had just happened.

"Ach, I'm truly sorry, Miss Eliza. It was such a grand evening. Perhaps tomorrow will bring a little more clarity." Daisy held her until her tears subsided. "Let me help ye to bed," Daisy said gently. Without another word, she assisted Eliza in changing and helped her into the comfort of the bed.

AFTER A RESTLESS NIGHT, Eliza rose at dawn. Looking at the sunrise casting light upon the stables and the surrounding area, she felt a little less gloomy. She recalled with pleasure the last few days and the connection she had felt with Thomas until overhearing the previous night's argument. How could he ask to continue to see her, and a few moments later admit to making such a vow?

She was confused and contemplated not what they had already found, but the loss of what might have been in the future. She hadn't felt this way before for someone and needed to protect her own heart and feelings. What a bitter conclusion to the Christmas celebration, and the continuing association of a man she cared for deeply—perhaps even loved. She sighed sadly, thinking of Ned and Pamela. *I will tuck those sweet memories away in my heart.*

Thoughts of the previous night jolted her into the task at hand. Her belongings were packed away and downstairs, ready for the awaiting coach. She glanced around the room one last time. The only signs of her presence were the book from the library, a wilted gardenia, and Thomas's clean handkerchiefs, left on a small table. As she entered the grand entryway, she saw Thomas and the children bidding the Saunders and Emmett goodbye. She held back until they had gone.

"Good morning, Eliza," Thomas greeted her, then frowned at her appearance. "Are you well?"

"Yes, I am well." She avoided eye contact, and fiddled with her gloves. "I had a difficult time sleeping last night." She could not reveal the true cause of her present state.

He said, pulling something from his vest pocket, "Kingsley found this earring. I recognized it as yours."

"Thank you," she replied, placing it in her purse. "It is my mother's and I am very grateful to Kingsley. I believe my father's coach has already arrived."

"Perhaps you would like to take a walk before you leave?" Thomas suggested.

"I need to be on my way. My family will be expecting me at home this morning." Looking at him directly for the first time, she said with a little more warmth, "Thank you for your hospitality, Thomas. Being here has been most enlightening." She hesitated and for a moment before continuing, "It has been most entertaining," she amended. "I hope you have a very Happy Christmas."

Thomas reached for her hand, which she quickly withdrew. She hugged each of the children before leaving. As she drove away, she saw Thomas and his children looking rather forlorn.

COMING ALONGSIDE HIS BROTHER, Daniel asked, "What just happened?"

"I have no idea. Last night everything was amiable between us. I asked if I could continue seeing her, to which she agreed. But this morning, her demeanor has completely changed. It was a daunting task for Miss Wentworth to even speak to me. Perhaps I am taking things too fast for her? We've only spent a few days together. It's possible she is entertaining reservations about me, being a widower with two children. I am completely baffled."

"But you have known each other for several years," Daniel countered.

"You would think that would count for something," Thomas said, scratching his head.

"YOU MEAN right after he asked to continue seeing you, you overheard Lord Bentley acknowledge he had made a vow never to marry again?" Margaret looked at Eliza as they sat in the sitting room at Wentworth Manor.

"How did you find this out?" Margaret asked, her brow furrowed.

"I heard it from his own mouth. After the ball, I went searching for a missing earring that had fallen off somewhere. While I was looking, I heard Thomas and Mr. Bentley in the study arguing. When I heard my name mentioned, I was curious to know why."

"Then what happened?" Margaret asked.

"Emmett Bentley accused his cousin of monopolizing my time and purposely keeping me away from him. He demanded to know what Lord Bentley's intentions were towards me."

"I assume Mr. Bentley is also interested in you?"

"Yes, we spent some time together." Eliza continued on, "Then Mr. Bentley brought up a vow Thomas had made to never marry again.

He asked him point-blank if he had made such a vow. Thomas admitted he had, and then refused to discuss it any further. He told his cousin it was none of his business. For a moment, I thought they might resort to fisticuffs. I ran to my room."

"No doubt in tears," Margaret said sympathetically.

"Thomas and his cousin discussing me as if I had no say in the matter, or not considering my feelings and desires, was very upsetting. After spending a perfect evening together, and Thomas asking to continue seeing me, I questioned if there was any future in it, and questioned his motives. Is he seeking a good friend's companionship or someone to be with his children? To continue in that manner, I would feel very dissatisfied and people would talk. I must have let my imagination take hold, pushing out common sense," Eliza concluded.

"It certainly does sound that way, the cad. You never should have been made to feel that way," Margaret said indignantly.

Mrs. Wentworth joined her daughters, and seeing Eliza, quickly lost her anticipation. "What is wrong, dear?" she asked.

"I can't talk about it right now, Mother. Margaret can tell you and Father later," Eliza said wearily, her eyes beginning to tear up.

"We'll talk about it when you're ready." Mrs. Wentworth hugged her daughter and exited quickly the way she came, a tear rolling down her cheek. As she left, a household maid appeared.

"Miss Wentworth, this just came for you." She handed Eliza a small, delicate box decorated with floral paper tied with ribbon and lace. Inside was a small cluster of white tea roses with a few tiny forget-me-nots carefully placed between the shimmering gold ribbon. Eliza read the note aloud.

Dear Eliza, Please accept my sincere apology for the stain on your lovely gown. I hope this corsage will hide the damage until it can be removed. I wish you a Happy Christmas and a prosperous New Year. Best Regards, Thomas Bentley.

"You didn't tell me about the stain," Margaret said.

"It really isn't important. Punch was accidentally spilled on my gown."

"Well, at least Lord Bentley is trying to make up for that!"

"I won't be wearing the dress or the corsage. Here, you can have it." Eliza thrust the box at Margaret and stomped out of the room.

HUDSON'S POND

*E*liza's seven-gore skirt swept the floor as she walked into the dining room. Before she was even seated, her father stood, shaking his fist.

"Eliza, I can't believe Lord Bentley would have so little regard for you. How dare he trifle with my daughter!" Mr. Wentworth shouted indignantly.

"Calm down, dear." Mrs. Wentworth took her husband's hand. "Things aren't always as bad as they appear. Eliza, do you think you should speak with Lord Bentley? Perhaps it's a misunderstanding. We could invite him for tea."

"Absolutely not. I don't want to pursue any further contact." She spoke more harshly than she had intended. "I'm sorry, Mother. I know you were just trying to be helpful."

"Eliza, would you care to join your father and me as we deliver our traditional English toffee to the neighbors?" Mrs. Wentworth asked.

"Thank you, Mother, but I'll just stay here," Eliza replied.

As her parents' coach pulled away, another coach pulled up to the manor. Eliza heard the ring of the bell and wondered who it could possibly be. If it were Lord Bentley, she couldn't decide whether the fluttering in her chest was from excitement or dread.

The butler announced, "Mr. Emmett Bentley."

Eliza breathed a sigh of relief when Emmett entered the room. Trotting along behind him was Winston, away from his usual place on a rug when guests arrived. Winston ran up to Eliza, wanting to be petted. After giving the dog the attention he wanted, Eliza said, "Mr. Bentley, how nice to see you."

"Good afternoon, Miss Wentworth." Emmett made a slight bow. "I wasn't able to say goodbye when you left Bentley Manor, and wanted to come today to wish you a Happy Christmas."

"Thank you, Mr. Bentley. How thoughtful of you." The argument she had heard between him and Thomas remained fresh in her mind. She was also aware of Emmett expressing his feelings of wanting to pursue her. The easiest way of dealing with it would be to proceed cautiously, as if nothing had happened.

"How is Admiral Saunders doing?" she asked.

"Much better. It seems he just needed his own bed and favorite chair."

"He sounds much like my father. He is happiest at home. I imagine Admiral Saunders appreciated your service."

"He said so, and I assured him that it was my pleasure to accompany them," Emmett replied with a winning smile.

Eliza concealed her astonishment at his reply, knowing that it was not entirely true. Doubts lingered about his sincerity and concern for others' feelings. In the midst of these reflections, Margaret and Lord Ainsley, on their way to take a walk, came into the room. As introductions were made and pleasantries exchanged, Eliza couldn't ignore Margaret's sly glance, wearing an expression that hinted, 'So this is Mr. Emmett Bentley.'

As Margaret and Lord Ainsley turned to leave, Eliza asked Margaret to see that Winston was taken to the servants' hall where he would be given a few scraps of food and some fresh water.

"Come, Winston," Margaret said. Winston followed her out, his tail wagging. "Eliza, why don't you show Mr. Bentley Father's new billiard table." Eliza was not terribly enthusiastic about her sister's suggestion, but felt not to do so now would be ungracious.

"Shall we, Mr. Bentley?" She led the way.

"By all means. I am fond of billiards, and have won a few games in my time," Emmett responded with enthusiasm.

Entering the parlor, she understood why her father wanted the alcove left empty. There, in the perfect spot for the tree, sat the billiard table. He was always full of surprises. At that moment, her father walked up and joined them. Eliza made the introductions.

"Do you play billiards?" Mr. Wentworth asked, watching Emmett admire the new acquisition.

"On occasion," Emmett said. "I usually play at my club. How nice you have one in your home."

"Shall we have a game?" Mr. Wentworth handed him a cue stick. "Perhaps we could make it more interesting with a small wager."

Eliza had no idea the game would involve money. Playing billiards and making a wager with someone you just met seemed out of character for her father. She watched as each man carefully plotted his shot. Her father showed a good deal of skill. Where had he learned to play so well? Was it while he was in London?

After a series of very competitive games, Emmett emerged the ultimate winner. "I'll need considerably more practice if I'm to win. against you," Mr. Wentworth admitted, handing him the money.

"You really don't have to, Mr. Wentworth." Emmett started to hand the money back. "But I do. It was a gentlemen's agreement," Mr. Wentworth insisted.

"Very well. A rematch would be fine anytime you wish. Better luck next time," Emmett said, his tone carrying a hint of condescension. It didn't sit right with Eliza that a guest in their home would be so insensitive.

The rudeness was gone as soon as Eliza noted it. Displaying his usual charm, Emmett thanked them for a delightful afternoon, and invited Eliza to go with him to Hudson's Pond the next day to go ice skating. She hesitated, not certain she wanted to be with Emmett again.

"The weather isn't too cold. And if you don't have skate blades, I'm sure I can find some somewhere around Bentley Manor." The mere mention of Bentley Manor brought a twinge of pain. Just when she felt she was making some progress, she'd slid back into her valley of disappointing dreams. She recognized that feelings can't be gone with a wave of a hand. It would take time and distance.

"That won't be necessary. I have my own blades. I'll dust them off and be ready tomorrow. Perhaps we can even have a race," she said confidently, eager to make up for her father's loss at billiards. It wasn't about a wager, but proving the Wentworths could hold their own, and showing Emmett she was as skilled at skating as he was at billiards.

Emmett gave a charming smile as he left. Standing in the main entryway, shaking her head, she found it impossible to dislike Emmett. His charm overrode his shortcomings.

"Congratulations on attracting another suitor." Margaret rushed up to Eliza. "He is very good-looking, and seemed quite taken with you." Margaret constantly encouraged her older sister to find a suitable companion and have the same happiness in marriage that she and Lord Ainsley had.

"He is dashing in his own way, but I don't see a long-range relationship in the future. There are certain qualities about him that bother me," Eliza confessed.

"Elizabeth Mae Wentworth, sometimes I wonder about your judgment. Give the man a chance! You have found fault with every man who has tried to pursue you, with the exception of Lord Bentley, who you are presently at odds with. You do not have to have everything figured out right away. Things usually work themselves out with time," her sister said with conviction.

Eliza recognized there was some truth to her sister's words.

"What do you think about Father's new billiard table?" Eliza diverted away from the previous conversation. "It must have been terribly expensive."

"I don't know the cost, only that Mother was appalled by it. She said it was an extravagance, and a waste of money, especially when she has been wanting to replace the worn-out drapes in some of the guest rooms. I guess we'll have to learn to play billiards," Margaret said. Eliza laughed, shrugging her shoulders.

SURELY SHE COULD MANAGE BEING ALONE on a short ride with Emmett to Hudson's Pond.

With Daisy away for the day, Eliza had no chaperone. However, everything was perfectly proper. Eliza sat on the forward-facing seat of the coach, while Emmett took the seat opposite her.

"Well, Mr. Bentley, are you ready for our race?" Eliza teased as they bounced along in the carriage.

"I must warn you, I am a fierce competitor. Are you up for it, Miss Wentworth?"

"I believe I am," she said confidently.

As they neared Hudson's Pond, a charming two-story home surrounded by evergreen trees came into view. Nearby, people leisurely sat on logs watching as skaters glided by. Smartly-dressed skating women in an array of fur muffs, velvet hats, and coats, added a touch of elegance akin to dancers on a stage. The men were no less impressive, wearing suits, crisp ties, and top hats or bowler hats. Some even carried a walking stick.

Near the edge of the pond, several people gathered around a young lad who was roasting chestnuts in a metal pan held over a fire encased in a metal container. This portable hearth, set on three legs, added a rustic touch to the winter scene.

It took a few minutes for Emmett to attach metal blades on Eliza's boots. While on one knee, he winked at her, his fingers lingering on the straps a bit longer than necessary. Eliza wondered if he was stalling for time before they raced, or was it something else entirely?

Holding hands, they soon joined the skaters, greeting many of their friends. She enjoyed seeing a skate sled pushed by a man in which sat a young lady, her face barely peeking out of a fuzzy hat tied under her chin like a baby bonnet. She recalled the joy of being in such a sled as a child with her father gliding her about. As she grew older, he taught her to skate, a passion she pursued regularly. Her father praised her skill and said she was exceptional on ice.

After circling the pond a few times, Emmett announced it was time for the race. He pointed out a log quite a distance away.

"The first one there is the winner," he declared. And they were off.

He pulled ahead at first, looking quite smug. Then she picked up speed, and pushed herself, skating faster than she had ever before. She was determined to win. Emmett was also, and lengthened his strokes. As they glided up to the log, she won by just a few inches, enjoying the victory and satisfaction of making up for her father's loss at billiards.

"Miss Wentworth, you amaze me. Hidden behind your fashion and style, is a real sportswoman. Well done!"

They took some time to catch their breath and sat eating roasted chestnuts and warming their hands by a fire. She recognized a pair of young men from church, Graham and Beckett, working hard. They added logs to the fire, along with joking and laughing with each other. An older man stood nearby, keeping a watchful eye on the two, ensuring their safety. The young men's light-hearted mood was a pleasure to see, and helped those around feel comfortable and at ease. The whole atmosphere was what made Hudson's Pond such a popular gathering place.

Those present were primarily from the immediate neighborhood, including many upper-class individuals. While social barriers still existed, they were somewhat relaxed in this setting, allowing a broader mix of skaters to enjoy the activities as well.

Emmett and Eliza left the warmth of the fire and stepped back onto the ice. As they did, a young lady skated by, teetered and fell. Observing proper ice-skating etiquette, Emmett quickly extended a helping hand and assisted the attractive young woman to her feet. The strands of her golden blond hair gleamed in the sunlight. With one arm supporting her, Emmett helped her limp off the ice.

"Poor thing," Eliza sighed, glad that it wasn't her.

She continued skating, enjoying herself until she realized Emmett had been gone an exorbitant amount of time. He was gone longer than she deemed necessary. Given his flirtatious nature, she couldn't help but wonder if he had become entangled in the long golden hair of the damsel in distress.

Perturbed, Eliza skated ahead not noticing a rut right in front of her. As she began losing her footing, she instinctively reached out grabbing at the air in a desperate attempt to keep her balance.

Suddenly from behind, a pair of strong arms encircled her waist just in time to prevent her from landing on the ice. Looking over her shoulder, Eliza saw a young man with the most piercing brown eyes she had ever seen. His gaze was intense, but inviting. He appeared to be slightly younger than her, and had a pleasant look about him.

"Are you steady now?" he asked, taking her hands and helping her stand straight.

"Yes, and thank you, kind sir," Eliza replied. "To whom am I indebted?"

"Louis Broadbent. I'm a nephew of Mr. and Mrs. Hudson, here for Christmas." His smile was warm and charming, with a hint of play-fulness.

"It is a pleasure, Mr. Broadbent. I am Miss Wentworth and I am here with a friend, who for now, seems to have disappeared. Fortunately, you came to my rescue in time."

"Miss Wentworth, I saw you on the ice presenting such a lovely picture until you hit the same rut that almost brought me down." Louis was still holding one of her hands.

"This young lady is with me," Emmett said abruptly as he skated up. He looked suspiciously at the young man.

"I beg your pardon, sir. I saw Miss Wentworth falling, and I caught her. It was the polite thing to do."

"He came to my rescue," Eliza interjected. The incident had begun to draw the attention of nearby skaters. Emmett sheepishly thanked the young man.

"Come join us for some chestnuts, Louis," a pretty young woman with dark curls and brown sparkling eyes called out. She was obviously family, by the shared good looks, and stepping in to rescue him from the awkward situation.

"With pleasure, Alicia," Louis replied, taking her hand. As they skated off, Louis tipped his cap, giving Eliza a parting smile, while avoiding eye contact with Emmett. The onlookers that had gathered dispersed.

"Was that really necessary, Mr. Bentley?" Eliza asked in a not-too-friendly tone. "The young man was only assisting me, much in the way you assisted the young lady who fell earlier on the ice."

Any romantic notions she had previously had vanished like smoke in the wind. She questioned whether he was prepared to keep focused on any one woman. The win on the ice could not make up for Emmett's actions. After the happenings of today, she was certain she did not want to spend more time with Emmett, and wished to return home.

Emmett, unaccustomed to being taken to task, made no comment, but suggested they remove their skate blades and watch the skaters. He quickly made his escape by going to fetch a blanket from the coach.

As Eliza sat waiting, her mood became somber. Then suddenly, two very excited children ran up to her, showering her with hugs.

"Ned, Pamela! What a wonderful surprise. I'm so happy to see you." Her eyes sparkled as she hugged both of them. Her dismal mood was transformed into elation. Soon, Pamela was perched on her knee and was bombarding her with excited chatter.

Eliza looked around for Thomas, and saw him heading her way. He looked handsome in his olive green corduroy coat and beige felt bowler hat. His appearance was reminiscent of the morning after the snowstorm when he had been outside helping clear the pathways. Oh, if only she could go back to that time. She pushed out the yearning feeling she had for him, knowing that rekindling the connection they once felt for each other was unwise.

"I do apologize, Eliza." Thomas leaned over and picked up Pamela. "Once the children saw you, there was no stopping them."

His imposing figure caused Eliza to be nervous as well as excited, her pulse racing. He was close enough that she could smell the pine scent of his soap. She had to take a deep breath, reminding herself that she was upset with him and was determined to remain aloof. But his disarming presence weakened her resolve. Trying to avoid being completely swept away by her feelings, she quickly turned her attention to the children as they bubbled with excitement about Christmas.

"Are your stockings ready to hang by the fireplace?" she asked.

"Yes. Since I'm bigger, my stocking is bigger than Pamela's," Ned bragged.

"There are some advantages to being the eldest," Eliza happily remarked, knowing each would use one of the stockings they normally wore with Pamela's being smaller.

Emmett returned with the blanket, frustration evident as he observed Eliza engrossed in conversation with Thomas and his children.

"What brings you to Hudson's Pond, Thomas?" Emmett asked as he walked up, his irritation barely concealed.

Thomas ignored his cousin's unfriendly greeting. "The children were getting restless and wanted to come watch the skaters. I am surprised to see you here with Miss Wentworth."

"We are just about to leave." Emmett unfolded the blanket, draping it over Eliza's shoulders as he helped her off the bench. "The air is getting chilly, and I don't want Eliza to get cold," he said protectively.

"No, that wouldn't do," Thomas agreed, his eyes narrowing slightly with a hint of suspicion in his gaze.

A bit saddened, but also grateful for the excuse to escape, Eliza gave each of the children a hug, and nodded to Thomas. Emmett managed to half-heartedly wish Thomas a pleasant afternoon.

The warmth of being inside the coach with the blanket wrapped around her, sipping warm cider, brought a measure of relief as Eliza grappled with her emotions. The feelings she had suppressed for Thomas emerged like struggling buds trying to make their appearance in the spring. Unwanted tears that came easily to her when she was upset or angry, started slowly sliding down her cheeks.

Rather than taking the seat across from her, Emmett sat beside her, reaching behind to adjust the blanket. "Miss Wentworth, are you well?"

"Yes, I am well. The cold air has made my eyes water," Eliza replied, regaining her composure and moving closer to the coach's window. Being with Thomas and the children evoked both joyful and melancholy memories of the time spent together. She realized how much she missed him. There was something wonderful about Thomas that she felt for no other man.

She removed the blanket from around her, deliberately creating more space between herself and Emmett. As the coach moved steadily toward her home, she tried to fill the silence with light-hearted chatter about Hudsson's Pond, her excitement for Christmas, and various other topics. Emmett responded with a few brief comments, seeming preoccupied with his own thoughts. Eliza tried to keep the conversation going, but eventually sat back and looked out the window.

After a prolonged silence, Emmett turned to her, took her hand and said, "Miss Wentworth, I enjoy your companionship very much, and would like to continue seeing you." His tone was determined and confident, as if there was no doubt about her acceptance. Eliza was startled by his declaration, realizing that her actions had encouraged him more than she had intended.

When Eliza faced Emmett with a questioning look, he said, "Surely, Miss Wentworth, you have suspected I care for you," he leaned closer to her. She stiffened and moved away, wishing Daisy was here. Why did Daisy have to pick today of all days to go to Bridgeview Hamlet to see her sister, Kate? Immediately, she felt a pang of guilt for her selfish thoughts. Daisy rarely took days off for herself.

"Mr. Bentley, I am sorry if I have misled you, which undoubtedly I have," she began, her voice reflecting some regret. "That was not my intention, but I must admit my uncertainty about my own feelings has affected you. I sincerely apologize. While we've shared a number of pleasant times together, I've come to see you as a friend," Eliza said kindly, but firmly.

To her way of thinking, today had been a pivotal day and she could not deny her true feelings, those endearing thoughts of Thomas, and the hugs from those two sweet children.

Emmett appeared shocked, then visibly disheartened. After a lengthy pause, he asked, "Is there someone else?"

Her silence was telling.

"If it is Thomas, I can assure you that it is not an easy road to travel, and could very well end in disappointment."

"Thank you, Mr. Bentley. I shall keep that in mind." She wasn't about to tell him she knew of Thomas's feelings on marrying again.

After a very uncomfortable ride, Wentworth Manor came into sight. Gathering up the shattered pieces of his pride, Emmett announced that he had been invited to spend the rest of the holiday with Admiral Saunders and his family, mentioning that he and the Admiral had become quite good friends. She thought she saw moisture in his gray-blue eyes.

"Happy Christmas," he said in a rather flat tone. Emmett spun on his heel and swiftly left, and Eliza had a feeling he wouldn't visit her again.

SETTING ASIDE PROTOCOL

"What has happened, Thomas? Are the children all right?" Daniel asked as Thomas came into the drawing room in a black cloud of dejection.

"The children are fine. Our ice-skating excursion was quite delightful until I saw Eliza with Emmett. I felt raging jealousy. Seeing her with him is driving me mad." He began to pace.

"Thomas, you must tell her how you feel," Daniel advised, sounding on the edge of exasperation.

"I only wish I could. When we discovered she was there, she hugged the children and was all smiles, and barely acknowledged me with a brief nod. She has made it very apparent she wants nothing further to do with me." He ran his hand through his hair.

"Do you have any idea of why she is avoiding you?" Daniel asked.

"No. The evening of the ball, we were enjoying each other's company. I felt an undeniable connection to Eliza and I believe she felt it as well. It was just one of those unexpected moments in your life when something happens that you do not easily forget. That is the reason that I find it even more perplexing that the next morning was such a contrast. She declined any attempt of my being attentive."

"Did anything happen after you said goodnight to her?" Daniel questioned.

Thomas paused. "Nothing involving Eliza. Emmett came to my study and we had an argument."

"About Eliza?"

Thomas hesitated. "Yes."

"Is it possible Eliza overheard your argument?" Daniel continued to probe.

"Possible, but improbable. If she did, it would be most unfortunate."

"Well, she doesn't appear to be avoiding Emmett's attention." Daniel looked directly at Thomas.

"I am aware of that, Daniel," Thomas said, clearly irritated with the whole matter. "Emmett is accustomed to getting whatever he wants. He clearly wants Eliza. Even though he is our cousin, I find him extremely annoying."

"But do women find him annoying? While in London, several ladies pursued him with no success. Now he is doing the pursuing, and his flamboyant ways may be more appealing than you give him credit for," Daniel pointed out.

Thomas could not deny the truth of that.

"Things have become complicated. My initial intention was to provide a Christmas gathering for our family and friends, a chance for us to settle into being in Amersham—nothing more. Rekindling my friendship with Eliza has brought on something I never expected," Thomas admitted. "She is so kind and thoughtful, and has a certain grace and elegance about her that I hadn't fully been aware of before. Seeing her again, I am struck not only by her warm personality, but her outward charm and beauty."

"You sound as if Miss Wentworth has opened your mind to the possibility of marriage. Thomas, my experience is that we don't always find love, love finds us." Daniel gave an all-knowing look.

"I would at least like the opportunity of finding out where this association might go, but when she sees me and basically ignores me, it is impossible. I find it all very confusing," Thomas grumbled. "We've had some quite personal conversations and moments of genuine happiness, and I have told her I enjoy being in her company."

"Trust me, brother, women love hearing such sentiments not just once, but often. By not speaking openly with Miss Wentworth, you're giving Emmett the advantage. Thomas, don't let this chance for happiness slip away," Daniel said.

"But how can I tell her? What if she is not interested and I fail?" Thomas's emotions were on edge.

"You can't fail or succeed if you don't try," Daniel insisted.

Thomas sat for a moment, deep in thought. Then his face brightened. "I have an idea."

THE SCENT of spices drifted through the kitchen from Eliza, her mother, and sister mixing up batches of their traditional, and undoubtedly favorite dessert: Christmas plum pudding.

From an early age, when they could be trusted to mix with a spoon without licking it, Mrs. Wentworth insisted her daughters learn how to prepare it. That way, they could continue the family tradition when they had families of their own.

Dressed in aprons, they had become cooks for the day with the kitchen staff enjoying seeing them invading their terrain.

"There, we're done," Margaret announced as she placed the last batch in the pantry. "All it needs now is to be topped with lemon sauce on Christmas Day."

Feeling sweaty and flushed from the heat of the oven, Eliza walked by the entryway in her soiled apron, wisps of hair falling on her face, and a smudge of flour on her cheek. Just then, the turn-key doorbell rang, and the butler swung the door open.

There he stood—unexpected, uninvited, and impeccably dressed in his brown tweed suit, which perfectly complemented his dark hair. She doubted her own eyes, knowing the importance Thomas placed on protocol.

She stood like a statue; her mind felt like a blank slate. In her apron, she looked more the part of a servant than a gentleman's daughter. She felt at a complete disadvantage. Finally she managed to say, "What are you doing here?"

"I beg your pardon for the intrusion, Eliza," he began, his gaze traveling over her from head to toe. Then his cheeks flushed and he looked flustered.

"I realize this is untoward," he said, handing his hat and gloves to the waiting butler, "but I have come to enlist your help. I'm on my way to town to choose toys for Pamela's and Ned's Christmas stockings. You have a knack of knowing what children like, and I don't want to disappoint them. Would you come with me? That is, if you can be spared from your baking duties." He arched an eyebrow.

"I can't possibly go." She cast him a disapproving look. "As you can see, I'm not properly dressed to go anywhere."

Just then Margaret walked up. She greeted Thomas in a very stand-offish manner, reflecting her protectiveness for her sister. Thomas stood his ground in spite of her cool reception and bowed slightly.

"Lady Ainsley, I understand congratulations are in order on the birth of your new daughter."

"Thank you, Lord Bentley," Margaret replied, her eyes narrowing slightly and her voice lacking warmth. The brief exchange highlighted the underlying tension, and her reluctance to extend further civility mirrored her disapproval of his visit.

Hearing voices in the foyer, Mrs. Wentworth appeared next. She invited Thomas into the sitting room, where he explained the reason for his visit. Eliza sat primly on a chair, determined to stay detached from the conversation, and determined to not to go with him.

It turned out that Thomas was as single-minded as she was, and kept up a pleasant conversation with her mother. Finally, Mrs. Wentworth turned to Eliza, something scheming in her eyes.

"Eliza, if you are willing to accompany Lord Bentley, you would be helping Cook. She told me this morning she hadn't realized she is out of cinnamon, and was in quite a dither. Given that there won't be any grocery delivery until after Christmas, you could save a stable hand from going into town. Daisy can come along as well, as a chaperone."

"Mother, I have already explained to Lord Bentley," she said as emphatically as she could, "I can't go with him in this state," she tugged at her apron, confident that would be the end of it.

"I am sure Lord Bentley will not mind waiting while you change. Would you, sir?" Mrs. Wentworth said in her sweetest voice.

"Not at all." He smiled pleasantly at Eliza, but she did not return his smile. In fact, she scowled as she tucked strands of hair back that had escaped from the combs holding them in place.

"While you change dear, I'll ring for tea," her mother said. Thomas gave Eliza an innocent look.

The nerve of that man! He knew exactly what he was doing. Obviously, though, Eliza did not want to cause a scene, so reluctantly agreed to go. As she left the room, she nearly collided with the maid, who was carrying a tray of tea, scones, and marmalade.

After Mrs. Wentworth and Thomas had consumed several cups of tea, Eliza returned.

Gone was the apron, replaced by an emerald green skirt with matching jacket, creating an air of understated elegance. A velvet hat, tilted just so, added a dash of adventure that hinted of her pleasant personality, which, for now, she kept carefully hidden.

"You look lovely, Eliza. Green suits you," Thomas said, standing and offering his arm, which she ignored. At this juncture, she erected a barrier to protect her own vulnerability.

Coming alongside her, Mrs. Wentworth whispered, "I've found it best to allow people the benefit of the doubt." Eliza shrugged, as if she had not heard her mother's words. She realized she was acting like a spoiled child. She really hadn't wanted to be so dramatic, but felt justified after being forced into doing something she did not want to do.

As they stepped outside, sunlit-clouds gracefully drifted across the clear blue sky while a light breeze toyed with the curls grazing Eliza's face. The temperature was moderate, a nice day for a coach ride.

Seeing Daisy standing next to the coach, Eliza breathed a sigh of relief. This would not be as difficult as she had thought.

"Daisy, it is such a pleasant day, would you care to sit with Mr. Edwards on the coachman's seat?" Thomas asked.

Eliza was flabbergasted. Having Daisy sit with Mr. Edwards outside the coach rather than inside, was highly unusual. The situation was vexing. What in the world was Thomas thinking?

What could they possibly talk about? She shuddered at the thought of yesterday's coach ride with no chaperone. That did not end well. Eliza felt trapped, yearning to return to the house. If only she could vanish like mist in the morning breeze.

Daisy blushed and smiled. With Mr. Edwards' assistance she was quickly sitting beside him with a blanket across her lap. He produced a wool scarf and cap, which he likely kept on hand for himself.

As the coach lurched forward, Eliza grasped onto the armrest and stared out the window avoiding eye contact with Thomas, who was seated opposite her.

Despite her attempts to snub him, Thomas spoke up.

"Eliza, I want to have a private conversation with you, hence no chaperone. Should you become uneasy, I will immediately tap on the coach's roof so Daisy can join us."

"Thank you," Eliza replied. She felt uneasy already.

"Did the corsage I sent you arrive?" Thomas asked.

"Yes, it was thoughtful of you," she replied in a flat tone.

"Please tell me something I need to know. The morning you left Bentley Manor, you made an interesting comment." Thomas looked directly at her, their knees nearly touching.

"I don't recall saying anything unusual?" she said, shifting uneasily in her seat. Leaning a little closer, Thomas pressed on.

"You said that being at Bentley Manor was most enlightening."

Eliza paused for a moment before saying, "I believe I corrected myself and said it had been most enjoyable."

"But you did say enlightening," Thomas persisted.

"I just misspoke." Eliza replied, folding her arms in front of her.

Thomas said in the kindest possible way, "When I walked you to your bedchamber door right after the Christmas Ball, you told me how much you enjoyed the evening. Then I mentioned wanting to continue seeing you, you agreed and said you would like that as well. However, the next morning you refused to take a walk, and acted very distant. I am puzzled by your change of heart and why there is a wedge between us."

She struggled fretting and twisting her fingers. Thomas waited patiently, the heavy silence between them becoming like an oppressive deep fog refusing to lift.

"Thomas, I want to be perfectly honest with you, even though I find this very difficult to talk about. Our families will have occasion to see one another, and I don't want to be the reason for discomfort when we encounter each other."

"Go ahead, Eliza. I think that is a good way to approach it," he said with a completely bewildered look on his face.

"Very well," she began slowly, keeping her voice steady. "On the night of the ball after you escorted me to my bedchamber door, I discovered I had lost an earring. While searching for it, through the partially open door of your study, I heard you and your cousin arguing. I had no intention of listening in on a conversation I was not privy to. However, when my name was mentioned, I was curious to know why."

"So you heard Emmett's accusations?" Thomas asked.

"Yes. I did. Inadvertently," Eliza replied.

Thomas put his hand on his forehead. "I'm so sorry you had to be subjected to such a conversation. That never should have happened," he said, apologetic. "What exactly did you hear?"

"Your cousin brought up a conversation you had in the past when you vowed never to marry again, that the pain of losing a wife was not worth the risk. You admitted to making that vow. I was terribly upset, not because I contemplated marriage, but because I thought we were more than friends. Then I wondered to what end?" She paused before continuing on.

"Perhaps I had mistaken our relationship for something more than it was. At that point, I forgot about the earring, and hurried back to my bedchamber." The tears she had managed to contain, began spilling down her cheeks. Reaching into her pocket for a handkerchief, she couldn't find one. Thomas passed his to her. She silently mouthed, 'Thank you.'

They both sat motionless as the coach wheels crunched intermittently over patches of snow, creating a faint squeaking sound that only added to the tension inside. Thomas moved next to her.

"Eliza, now I can understand why your attitude toward me changed. Hearing what you did, my behavior toward you would appear ungentlemanly. When I heard those accusatory words from Emmett, I had to restrain my anger, and control a desire to cuff him right then and there. Please believe me, I would never do anything to hurt you, or expose you to anything that could tarnish your reputation. Be assured, my intentions are honorable. If you will allow me, I will tell you the part of the conversation you did not hear."

She nodded and continued dabbing her eyes.

"First of all, Emmett accused me of purposely arranging to have him leave with Admiral Saunders and his family, to keep him from further contact with you. I explained that Miss Saunders made that request. She was uneasy about leaving without additional help with her father, who was suffering from an old battle wound. I left it up to Emmett. If he did not wish to go, I would have given a reasonable excuse and had a footman go in his place."

Eliza had stopped crying, and was less tense, her features softening.

"As for the other part of our conversation, I admitted openly that I had made a vow never to marry again, and refused to discuss the subject further. That part you heard. The next part is what you did not hear. I relented, and went on to explain to Emmett that I made that vow over a year ago while living in London. While there, I had met several women more interested in my title and money than in me or my children. As a result, I became wary of pursuing marriage."

Eliza sat stunned. "You are not opposed to marrying again, should the opportunity arise for you?"

"Not at all," he assured her.

Eliza smiled at Thomas, visibly relieved. "I was unsure what to make of it, especially after spending such a pleasurable evening with you looking forward to more. I am sorry for misjudging your intentions. It seems we've both been caught up in a misunderstanding, and I appreciate that you've made this effort to resolve it." The defense she had built up around her fell away like fallen leaves being scattered by the wind. This was the second time in two days she had a serious conversation with a man. How had her life become so complex?

"Hearing what you did, I understand your reaction," he said, his voice taking on a tone of genuine understanding and empathy.

She brightened and said with earnestness, "You expressed a desire to continue seeing me. If that is still your wish, that is mine as well."

"Yes, I would like that very much," Thomas drew her close. "Returning to Amersham and being with you is the best thing that could have happened to me, but I questioned if you wanted to be with a widower with two children. Was that a situation you would want to deal with? I felt, perhaps, that was the reason you distanced yourself."

"Thomas, I adore your children." Eliza's eyes sparkled as she spoke, her voice filled with genuine affection.

"The children, in turn, love you. Pamela was in tears when you left, and Ned moped around all morning. Then there is the matter of Emmett." His brow furrowed. "I have been tormented by thoughts that you prefer him." Thomas's honesty was unexpected. She dropped his hand and gently touched his cheek.

"Your cousin is a friend, nothing more. He asked to continue seeing me, but I declined. As I spent more time with you, my admiration grew—your attentiveness to your children, the capable and personal way you oversee the manor, and the way you are able speak on a variety of subjects." She paused and blushed, "And I do find you rather attractive."

"Only rather attractive?" Thomas teased, raising an eyebrow and a mischievous grin. He was clearly charmed by her coy look and her sparkling eyes, appearing emerald green against the lovely green outfit.

"Very attractive," she admitted softly, surprising herself with her own boldness. With that, she nestled her head against his shoulder. He gently rested his forehead against her temple.

"Just being with you again, Eliza," Thomas said, "I was not only reminded of your beauty, but of the many qualities I love about you— your talents, your caring nature, and your strength. Seeing you at Hudson's Pond made me realize it was time to act on my feelings."

"I am so glad you did," she replied. "That same day, when I unexpectedly saw you and Ned and Pamela, I was overwhelmed with a longing to be with all of you again. I have tried pushing those emotions aside, with no success."

"From this point, I hope we can move forward," Thomas said with relief in his voice.

A memory of Julia flickered in her mind and Eliza sat up with a start. "How can I even consider furthering our relationship? I could never take Julia's place. I have too much love and respect for her memory." Her voice wavered, tears welling up again.

"Eliza, you would not be taking her place, or showing disrespect in any way," Thomas responded gently. "Julia will always be a part of my life, as well as the children's. Her gracious and loving manner is something I treasure, and hold in a permanent place in my heart. We had two beautiful children, and then she passed, and my life changed dramatically. I told the children that she has gone to be with the angels, and I truly believe that in my heart. Since then, there has been happiness, especially through the children, though I have faced difficulties and loneliness. But when I least expected it, a door to happiness opened. I became reacquainted with you. I have discovered why Julia treasured your friendship so highly. I want to be with you for who you are."

She sat silently for a few moments, absorbing the weight of his words before turning to face him. "My doubts have vanished," she finally said, her voice filled with sincerity. "To know that you value me for myself brings a happiness that is difficult to express. Thomas, I am thrilled with the thought of being with you as we discover more about each other, and your children."

His gaze dropped to her full lips, and his own beckoned to be kissed. As they leaned towards each other, a sudden jolt of the coach threw them off balance. They both laughed as they righted themselves, realizing that they were on a very bumpy part of the road. Their first kiss was for now postponed.

"I have been such a ninny," Eliza said, leaning back against his shoulder as he played with a lock of her hair.

"Befuddled, but not a ninny," Thomas laughed. "However, I suggest that the next time you are eavesdropping...."

"I was not eavesdropping," she countered, "I happened upon a conversation."

"Well, the next time you happen upon a conversation, I suggest you see the thing through. I hope that not a whisper, worry, or problem of this nature will ever mar your lovely brow again," he added, his hand finding hers and giving it a reassuring squeeze.

"You are a clever one, Thomas Bentley," she stated.

"How so?" he asked.

"Not only have we had an intimate conversation, but Daisy and Mr. Edwards have been able to spend time together."

"I try to be mindful of my staff's needs," Thomas said dryly. "But there is one thing I am certain of," he added with a smile. "I must always carry two handkerchiefs—one for you and one for me."

THINGS SORTED OUT

*A*s Thomas and Eliza stepped from the coach, they were smiling and walking together in a very companionable way.

"Mr. Edwards, stable the horses at the Swan Inn and you and Daisy take refreshments. Meet us back here in an hour," Thomas said, tossing up a money pouch.

"Very good, sir," Mr. Edwards responded with a grin on his face as he flicked the reins and the horses moved forward.

Thomas and Eliza entered the bustling mercantile, which seemed oddly quiet. The sparse amount of customers, Eliza speculated, could be a result of people staying at home preparing for Christmas Day.

Despite the mishmash of merchandise on every shelf, Mr. Gardner, the proprietor, knew where everything was located. His motto was, 'If we don't have it, we will get it for you.'

He was at the counter, helping a customer, wearing a flour-sack apron over his simple attire. One long dark strand of his hair had slid down on his forehead revealing his attempt to cover a bald spot. Tyler, his red-headed son, was dressed in a well-tailored shirt and trousers, likely in an attempt to impress the young ladies.

"Good day, Lord Bentley, Miss Wentworth. How can I be of service?" Mr. Gardner asked.

"Good day to you as well, Mr. Gardner. Has the rocking horse I had ordered arrived yet?" Thomas inquired.

"Yes, Lord Bentley, it's here, and a sight to behold. The wood glider-base is much safer than the previous rocking horses. It even has a padded seat," Mr. Gardner explained, motioning to his son.

"Tyler, fetch the rocking horse Lord Bentley ordered!"

"Yes, sir," Tyler replied before disappearing behind a curtain near the back of the store. "Miss Wentworth has agreed to help me pick out a few toys for my children's stockings. Could you point us in the right direction?" Thomas asked.

"Certainly." Mr. Gardner led them to the shelves displaying toys and such. Then he discreetly busied himself straightening a nearby shelf. But his attention was fixed on Thomas and Eliza.

Perhaps a hint of Christmas magic filled the air as Eliza and Thomas perused the store, enjoying one another's company, oblivious to what was going on around them.

Eliza exclaimed, "Oh, Lord Bentley, come look at this kaleido-scope. I think Ned and Pamela would both like this."

As she turned the kaleidoscope to view several colorful patterns, she sensed Thomas had walked behind her. He stood close and whispered in her ear, "I adore you." His mind was definitely not on kalei-doscopes.

She felt a thrill as he stood so near that she could feel his breath. She wanted to turn around so he could kiss her, but certainly she did not want their first kiss to be in the mercantile. Not only would it be inappropriate, but it would also lack romance. Instead, she reached back, took his hand and squeezed it. Seeing Tyler returning through the curtains carrying a rocking horse, they quickly drew apart.

Thomas carefully inspected the beautifully crafted wooden rocking horse. The intricate painted designs on the saddle and bridle, the mane and tail adorned with horse's hair, and the eyes painted life-like with a gentle gaze, gave it a playful look.

"Very nice, even finer than I expected," Thomas said. "This undoubtedly will become a favorite addition to the nursery."

"I wanted you to see it before we detach the glider, and wrap it in burlap so it can be safely transported to Bentley Manor," Mr. Gardner said with satisfaction. The rocking horse and packages of toys Eliza found were tucked into the leather boot of the coach. Once they were underway, Daisy glanced occasionally at Eliza and Thomas, who were whispering sweet nothings to each other.

When Mrs. Wentworth greeted Eliza and Thomas, she was startled at the change in her daughter's countenance. Thomas asked to speak with Eliza's father privately. As he walked toward the study, Eliza said quietly to her mother and Margaret she would explain everything after Thomas left. A few minutes later, Thomas and Mr. Wentworth emerged from the study, talking cordially and shaking hands.

"What did you and Father talk about?" Eliza asked, as Thomas prepared to leave.

"Oh, the stock market and the price of horses," he teased. Seeing her impatience, he took her hand, "We discussed my intentions toward you."

"And what did you say?" She cocked her head to one side with a coquettish look.

"I assured your father that my intentions are entirely proper, and I wish to court you. That is, if you are agreeable to that arrangement."

"Yes, Thomas, yes." Her eyes sparked with delight. Standing together in the foyer under a small chandelier, Thomas pointed up to a bundle of greenery with mistletoe overhead.

"Where did that kissing ball come from?" Eliza said, suspecting it was Margaret's doing.

"Remember, Eliza, it's a tradition to exchange kisses under the kissing ball to strengthen the continuation of our delightful association," Thomas said softly.

"Do you believe that?" she asked.

"Absolutely! When it involves kissing, why quibble with tradition?" Cupping her face in his hands, he leaned down and kissed her. Then he took her into his arms and kissed her again. She wrapped her arms around his neck, feeling the soft strands of his hair at the nape. His kisses were everything she had imagined and more.

"Two kisses in one day," she said, leaning back in his arms, and smiling.

"Scandalous!" Thomas chuckled, before letting himself out and closing the door behind him.

Eliza practically floated into the room where her mother and sister sat anxiously waiting to speak with her.

Margaret immediately asked, "What has caused this transformation between you and Lord Bentley?"

"Well," Eliza began, "Thomas explained that the night of the Christmas Ball, I had only heard part of the conversation he had with his cousin."

"He didn't deny saying he vowed never to marry again, did he?" Margaret questioned, still retaining some suspicion. She noted Eliza's use of Thomas's given name.

"No, not at all. He admitted he had made such a vow. Then he told me of the last part of the conversation that I did not hear. Thomas said he set Mr. Bentley straight—that he had made that vow over a year ago, and no longer had those feelings. Thomas had no idea I had overheard them, and was at a loss as to why I had left in such a huff the next morning."

The three of them sat for a few moments, while her mother and sister processed the new information.

"With the misunderstanding behind us, Thomas has informed Father that it is his intention to court me." Eliza blushed and clasped her hands together.

"That is wonderful, Eliza. I knew there was something amiss all along," her mother declared with some satisfaction. "He is too much of a gentleman to act in such a cavalier manner."

"Thank you, Mother, for your advice," Eliza said and kissed her mother on the cheek.

"I'm sorry I called him a cad." Margaret squirmed in her chair. "I am happy for you, Eliza."

Mr. Wentworth joined the ladies, with Winston following close behind. Winston ran up and put his paw on Eliza's skirt, looking for attention. "Winston, even you are happy about my good news," she said, bending over and scratching him behind his ears.

"I have no doubts about Thomas's intentions, Eliza, and I am very pleased to give my support to your courtship," her father stated proudly.

"What a joyous holiday this is proving to be," Mrs. Wentworth said. "Eliza, I have an idea. Would you like to invite Lord Bentley and his family to join us tomorrow for Christmas dinner?"

"Mother, I'm so glad you thought of that," she replied excitedly.

"I will send Hunter, our most reliable footman and fastest rider, to deliver the invitation," Mrs. Wentworth decided.

Eliza gasped, then groaned, covering her face with her hands.

"What is it, dear?" her mother asked.

"I forgot to get the cinnamon!"

AN ALMOST PERFECT CHRISTMAS

" $\mathcal{H}$ urry, Eliza, or we will be late for church," her father called. "We don't want to miss the Christmas service."

"Coming, Father." She joined him, hastily putting on her leather gloves. The rest of the family were already seated in the coach. *Fashionably late, as usual*, she thought as they got underway. As they neared the church, she could hear the peeling of church bells. Eliza always loved the sound of bells, especially on Christmas morning. The tones of peace and goodwill rang out with each clang and rattle.

Numerous coaches and carriages were depositing their passengers outside the church. A swell of people greeted each other with handshakes and hugs. Among them was Dr. Dyer and his wife and two daughters, Breanna and Lindsey. Eliza, always aware of fashion, smiled when she saw the lovely velvet pastel-hued bonnets trimmed with ribbons and dainty lace the young ladies were wearing. She felt a twinge of guilt as Dr. Dyer tipped his hat to her. She determined it was time to tell her parents about assisting Dr. Dyer.

Seeing Thomas, Eliza hurried along toward the church's door. His smile brightened at the sight of her, and he warmly greeted the family. "Would you care to join the Bentleys in a pew? My brother's family and my children are already inside."

"Certainly. Happy Christmas, Lord Bentley," her father responded.

"To you as well, Mr. Wentworth," Thomas said.

Eliza and Thomas slid in first with their respective families seated on either side.

"I'm unaccustomed to being seated next to a gentleman." She shifted in her seat.

"I suggest you get used to it, for I plan to have you sitting by my side as often as possible." Her cheeks flushed a delicate pink as he gently squeezed her hand. Eliza watched as Pamela, doll in hand, scooted past her father, and climbed onto her lap. Eliza held her close and gently rocked her. Before long, Pamela was asleep. Eliza felt she had been given a Christmas gift, having this precious little girl in her arms.

Eliza then felt another twinge of guilt when her eyes settled on Dr. Dyer.

"What is wrong?" Thomas whispered.

After a moment, she finally admitted, "I believe it is time to tell my parents about my true situation with Dr. Dyer. But I am afraid of my father's censure."

"Your father seems like an understanding man. I suspect he will not be offended by your actions, especially when he realizes how generous you are with your time and skills."

"I will tell him as soon as we return home," she murmured, then remained quiet for the rest of the service.

"Did you notice that neither your cousin or the Saunders family are here today?" Eliza asked as they strolled slowly to the waiting coach. Thomas commented that he had, and informed her Emmett had visited him the night before.

"Emmett was full of apologies for his ungentlemanly behavior and asked if we could be friends again. He admitted his accusations were unfounded, and were driven by pride. Acknowledging that being an only child and getting everything he wanted had made him self-centered, he admitted it was time to stop blaming his behavior on that and make amends. I decided not to mention that you overheard our argument."

"Were you surprised by his visit?" Eliza asked.

"I was. It took a great deal of humility on his part to be so contrite. To resolve misunderstandings, especially at Christmastime, is something I truly appreciate. After all, we are family, and I want our association to be pleasant and amiable." Eliza was touched by Thomas's forgiving nature.

"When we come over this afternoon, Pamela would like to bring her new kitten, Snowball. It seems they are inseparable."

"I'm sure we can accommodate Snowball," Eliza laughed.

Waiting by the coach for a few more minutes, Thomas kissed Eliza's hand. "Until this afternoon," he said. She was drawn to the dimple in his chin and couldn't resist touching his face, a beautiful smile gracing her lips.

As Eliza and her family rode along in the coach, she remained silent. When her mother asked if anything was wrong, Eliza assured her she was fine, though nervously biting her lip. After they returned home, Eliza casually requested to speak with her father privately.

Closing the study door behind them, her father said, "Things appear to be going well with you and Lord Bentley."

"Yes. We are very happy," Eliza replied. "What I would like to talk to you about concerns me."

"Go on, dear. What is it?"

"I must confess, Father, that I have been secretly assisting Dr. Dyer on his visits. I don't like keeping this from you and mother, but learning nursing is something I value deeply. I've had an interest in nursing since I was a child. Please know that my dedication to this doesn't diminish my love and commitment to our family. I have no excuse for my behavior except the satisfaction of being of service. Please forgive me, Father. I detest being dishonest with you. It was all my doing, and Dr. Dyer only agreed to it because of my pleading."

Her father raised his hand to his forehead, shaking it side to side. He appeared quite distraught, a grave look on his face, reflecting his inner turmoil as if there were more pressing matters that he dared not share.

"I am so sorry this has upset you so, Father. I would never want that, particularly on Christmas Day," she said, offering comfort.

"This is my fault too. I should have been more supportive and encouraged you to pursue your desires. I, too, have a confession. Actually, I have known about this for some time. An acquaintance of mine, Mr. Heath Harvey, told me that while he was visiting his sister, Dr. Dyer was treating her son, and that you were there, too. I had some suspicions that something was afoot when you would leave the house dressed more simply than usual."

"Father, I should have come forward sooner," Eliza lamented.

"I felt you would tell me when you were ready."

"Thomas was right," she continued, "you are understanding."

"Lord Bentley—is he aware of your assisting Dr. Dyer?" her father asked.

"Yes, I confided in him during the Christmas celebration at his home. Today, he noticed something was bothering me. When I told him what it was, he encouraged me to tell you. I promise, Father, there will be no more secrets!"

Her father flinched.

"Father?" Eliza queried, concerned. "Are you well?"

"Just some arthritis. Nothing for you to be worried about." Mr. Wentworth's laugh sounded nervous, but Eliza attributed it to his arthritic pain.

THAT AFTERNOON, the Bentleys arrived for Christmas dinner. Thomas expressed his pleasure at seeing Eliza wearing the gown she had worn the night of the Christmas ball, with the corsage strategically placed over the stains.

"The plum pudding was delicious," Lily remarked. "I believe it is the best I have ever eaten."

"It's been a family favorite for years. My daughters and I tradition-ally prepare it." Mrs. Wentworth spoke with satisfaction. Thomas made no attempt to stifle his laugh, recalling his unexpected visit the day of baking. Eliza looked at him with feigned annoyance, arching an eyebrow.

Moving into the parlor, they were pleased to see that Winston's initial hesitation and barking due to the presence of Snowball had mellowed. The two had settled into a peaceful coexistence. Snowball was nestled on a plush pillow on an ottoman, while Winston stretched out nearby, keeping watch on his new feline friend. The footman, who had been watching over them, exited the room.

Blind Man's Bluff and Change Seats, filled the room with bursts of laughter and squeals. Charades concluded the game-playing, and shortly after, Margaret and Lord Ainsley exchanged glances before excusing themselves.

"I'm afraid Victoria had us up several times during the night," Margaret said with a weary smile. "Even with her nursemaid, she would only settle down with me. We need to get some rest."

Sitting near the hearth with the Yule log burning, Pamela, Ned, and Abigail were intrigued by an interlocking wooden puzzle. Before long they had matched the pieces that formed a woodland scene complete with a deer, a rabbit, and an owl perched on a tree.

"Would you gentlemen care to play a game of billiards?" Mr. Wentworth proudly pointed to his newest acquisition.

Thomas, picking up a cue stick, tried it out on the red ball. He and Daniel had played before and were eager to play. As the men removed their waistcoats, Eliza couldn't help but notice the impressive breadth of Thomas's shoulders when he rolled up his sleeves. The evidence of his strength caught her admiring gaze.

Eliza's heart danced as she observed the scene. Thomas's smile, laughter, and easy banter blended effortlessly with the others. He was already becoming a valued part of her family circle. She wondered why she had ever encouraged Emmett's attention. Thomas had all the attributes she admired. As he moved around the billiards table, his gaze occasionally shifted to her, offering a warm smile that spoke volumes, a look that only the eyes of love can see.

The red, yellow, and white balls were soon bumping around the table like pebbles being kicked about.

"That's a foul, Thomas," Daniel announced as the white ball slipped up the side of the table and onto the floor. "I won," he declared triumphantly.

"Very well, I concede." Thomas returned his cue stick. His waistcoat remained on a nearby chair.

Eliza then watched Thomas play a rousing game of marbles with Ned, crouched down in his shirttails, still looking handsome as ever. He seemed so carefree, Eliza found herself watching him with a silly smile all afternoon.

With Pamela dozing on his shoulder, Thomas was the last to leave. He leaned over and kissed Eliza without disturbing his sleeping daughter or her kitten. "Eliza, this has been a perfect Christmas," Thomas said.

"Well, an almost perfect Christmas." A hint of concern showed on her face.

"What are you referring to?"

"My father was visibly upset when I told him about my service with Dr. Dyer, even though he admitted he already knew about it. I just don't understand," Eliza said.

"Often men can be sensitive about their children working, especially a daughter of your social status. It is something he is definitely not used to," Thomas offered, his tone comforting. She went up on her tiptoes, and gave him a playful kiss on the cheek.

"Thank you, Thomas, that must be what it is. Tomorrow's the First Day of Christmas. I'm looking forward to spending it with you."

"Until then, my dear Eliza," he said, "good night and sweet dreams."

Shutting the door, she stood in the hall, reflecting on what a delightful Christmas it had been—one she would always treasure. Later that evening, she told her mother about the conversation she had earlier in the day with her father.

"I wished I had waited until after Christmas to tell him."

Mrs. Wentworth expressed her concerns that her husband had not been sleeping well and didn't seem quite himself. At her insistence, he had finally agreed to see Dr. Dyer. This was the first time Eliza had heard of this. She hoped Thomas was right about her father's reaction, but feared her father's behavior might indicate a deeper issue. Was it his health, or was there something else?

THE TWELVE DAYS OF
CHRISTMAS

*A*s the first rays of post-Christmas sunlight streamed through the window, Eliza felt the excitement in the air. With the New Year's gala invitation in hand, anticipation and joy welled up within her. She was thrilled to spend the First Day of Christmas, December 26, and the days that followed, with Thomas and his children. She couldn't wait for the delightful ice cream-tasting excursion in Amersham planned for later that afternoon.

"Mother, can I help you fill the boxes you're giving out today?" Eliza offered as she joined her mother in the dining room, where boxes filled with food and gifts sat on the large dining room table. Distributing these boxes to the staff was one of her mother's favorite traditions. It gave her the opportunity to express the family's appreciation of their service. Many were given the day off to spend with their families, while others would work only part of the day.

"I have prepared a special box for Dr. Dyer that contains treats, as well as a lovely Afghan blanket and a thank you note for mentoring you. He has definitely had an impact on your life, and your father and I want him to know we appreciate that."

"Thank you, Mother, that's so thoughtful of you," Eliza responded gratefully. "I am certain Dr. Dyer will be happy to learn of yours and

Father's approval of my assisting him." Eliza was constantly amazed at her mother's efforts to think of others.

"Eliza," Mrs. Wentworth continued, "would you fill the Christmas cards with money? There is a stack of shillings and half-crowns with a list of how much each person is to receive." Her mother pointed to a spot on the table.

She picked up a Christmas card depicting a young boy and a girl adorned in pristine white coats, their cherubic faces reminding her of Ned and Pamela. They stood side by side, the girl gently cradling a small fir tree in her arm, while the boy held a large paper cone with a variety of toys sticking out. They seemed to be the embodiment of the enchantment that Christmas brings to children.

Her thoughts suddenly shifted to Thomas, and she wondered if he felt the same longing for her as she did for him. Patience was her only recourse, a virtue she found challenging. Resolving to be more patient would be one of her New Year's resolutions. As she considered this possibility, her thoughts took a detour back to Thomas again.

"Oh well," she mused, as she placed coins in the envelope and signed the card, "I'll begin that resolution on January first."

The day seemed to move as slowly as molasses, each minute stretching out like taffy. Finally, it was time for Eliza to travel with Thomas and the children to the new ice cream parlor. Ned and Pamela were excited, discovering that the shop offered a variety of desserts.

The owner, Mr. Rinaldi, and his family had recently arrived from Italy to Amersham, bringing with them treasured family recipes. Choosing between vanilla, chocolate, strawberry, or a fruit-based flavor was overwhelming to Ned and Pamela. In the end, chocolate won out.

"Papa, it's yummy. I love it!" Pamela exclaimed, as she savored the last bite from her glass dish. Ned was too engrossed in his ice cream to say anything.

Mr. Rinaldi, speaking English with a charmingly broken accent, explained to Thomas's inquiry of how the ice cream was kept cold. His enthusiasm was evident.

"Ice it is hauled over from frozen pond nearby and put in big wooden box with straw inside," Mr. Rinaldi explained. "That keep ice cream cold for much days. I plan to build proper ice house this spring."

This was a perfect start of the Twelve Days.

The next few days overflowed with festive activities, from a lively gathering at the town hall for a potluck, to intimate moments at home sharing cherished holiday stories and popping popcorn in a cast iron pan in the fireplace. Ned and Pamela squealed with delight one afternoon as they all went sledding, accompanied by Winston who went bounding through the snow alongside the children as they slid down the hill. Mrs. Adams had sent along biscuits and apple cider.

One evening consisted of an invitation to a friend's home—Henry and Alexis Kensington—where the air was filled with lively music. The Kensington family were quite the musicians and had included several friends to join them.

Whether at the Wentworth residence or Bentley Manor, each day brought new joy as Eliza and Thomas spent their first holiday season together. Amidst the festive activities, they were drawn to each other with increasing warmth and affection, sharing laughter and stolen glances. Eliza found being with Thomas and the children felt natural, and it was becoming increasingly difficult to be apart.

As Thomas and Daniel sat in the library one evening, Daniel couldn't resist asking, "So, Thomas, when are you going to propose to Eliza?"

"Is it that obvious?" he asked, trying to act nonchalant.

"Yes, it is quite evident that's where things are headed."

Thomas sighed. "There are some things we need to talk about, but finding time we can be alone is a challenge."

"Lily and I have been talking about doing something just for the children. Tomorrow, while Eliza is here, we will entertain them in the nursery. Lily plans to read *Alice's Adventures in Wonderland* to them and afterward have a Mad Hatter tea time, complete with funny hats.

She wants me to wear a ridiculous oversized green polka dot bow tie with a silly hat of various colors, complete with a feather sticking out. I only agreed to do it to help your cause," Daniel teased with a half-cocked smile.

"There you go, little brother, looking out for me again," Thomas laughed, giving Daniel a friendly pat on the shoulder.

"Well to be fair, it wasn't all my idea. Lily remembers how hard it was to have a few moments alone before we were engaged."

THE FOLLOWING AFTERNOON, Eliza and Thomas were savoring tea in the conservatory. This was fast becoming her new favorite room. It was as delightful in the daytime as in the evening. The large windows allowed soft sunlight to play throughout the room, as well as a peaceful sense of connection with the natural world outside. The delicate sweet scent of a winter-blooming jasmine enhanced the romantic atmosphere. A perfect spot for a proposal.

"It seems unusually quiet." Eliza's teacup clattered on the saucer.

"I have given the staff the afternoon off," Thomas said. "I managed to convince Mrs. Adams that we could fend for one evening for ourselves. However, she insisted on leaving a prepared meal and a housemaid."

"You are very brave," Eliza replied drolly. "Where are the children?"

"Daniel and Lily are with them in the nursery. I wanted us to have some time alone."

"Oh, for any particular reason?" She shifted in her chair, her eyes locking onto his with a glimmer of anticipation. She was ready for the romantic conversation she sensed was about to unfold.

"Eliza," Thomas began, "I know you enjoy being in London. How would you feel about establishing a residence there?"

Eliza was taken aback. That was not the question she expected. Maybe it was his way of leading to something more? "I suppose it depends on who I am with," she responded.

"Well, me, of course," Thomas said, running his hand through his hair.

Eliza looked up, her blue eyes sparkling, full of curiosity. "That sounds intriguing. What exactly do you have in mind?"

Taking her hand he said, "If we were to wed, we could divide our time between Amersham and London." She contemplated its implications and where the conversation might lead. Was he just trying to see if she were open to such a suggestion? She had never thought of moving to London.

"Such an arrangement has practical merit," Thomas added, his tone matter-of-fact. Eliza drew her hand back in surprise and began fidgeting with her fingers intertwining and twisting them in a familiar, nervous manner. Her mind raced for a reply, and the first thought that came to her was the availability to learn more about medicine and nursing. Eliza hesitated to say anything, choosing to reserve her words until there was an actual marriage proposal.

He shifted to discussing the merits of the city. "I would be able to conduct my business with greater efficiency. Ned could attend a private school, and you could shop to your heart's content. As much as you like being outdoors, you could learn to ride a bicycle. Women are wearing those new-fangled walking skirts that button in front for easier riding."

"I actually have one of those skirts, and wore it when I went tobogganing with your brother's family," she replied. Eliza pointed an accusatory finger at him. "You're trying to divert my attention from the real issue of accompanying you in London."

This conversation was not the heart-stopping one she had conjured up in her mind—with him on bended knee, declaring his undying love for her. In contrast, she felt like they were discussing one of his investments. It seemed he was circumventing the question, or perhaps uncertain how to approach the matter. Rarely at a loss for words, he was floundering.

It all came to an abrupt end when Pamela ran into the room. "Papa, look! Abigail taught me how to do a somersault," she said excitedly, and promptly got down and did one slightly off-center.

"That's wonderful, dear," Thomas laughed, picking her up. "We will continue this conversation later," he whispered to Eliza and gave her a quick kiss on her cheek.

After returning home, Eliza struggled to concentrate on anything. What had once been a bright and hopeful topic now hung heavily over her like a rain-soaked cloud. She wondered what Thomas was waiting for. He had broached the subject of marriage, but he hadn't provided a clear declaration. Their time spent together hadn't been extensive, yet it was evident that they were moving towards marriage.

A courtship lasting a year or more, like most of her friends, was not realistic. In her heart she wanted to be with Thomas. She wanted to be his wife—care for his children. Although she would be their stepmother, she already loved them like her own. Her feelings for Thomas were unlike anything she had previously felt, and she could envision herself spending the rest of her life with him. Grateful that she had not been a victim of an arranged marriage, or been engaged to someone prior to getting to know them on a deeper level, Eliza thought about the conversation she had with Thomas and his implied but unspoken words.

When will he propose? The next time they would be together was the next day, on New Year's Eve. Knowing he guarded his privacy, it would never happen in such a public setting. Maybe on New Year's Day, or the day after. Her mind was swirling with questions. She was determined not to let doubts subdue her positive thoughts.

In the past, whenever she was about to undertake something new and important, fear would creep in like an unwanted guest. She would replace fear with faith—faith in Thomas and in herself. After all, she reasoned, she was capable of making a wise decision when it presented itself. She had imagined when he would propose and rehearsed what she would say. Yet, the moment of his proposal remained shrouded in mystery, leaving her to wonder when and where it would actually come about.

A NEW YEAR'S SURPRISE

On New Year's Eve, Thomas arrived at Wentworth Manor dressed impeccably in black tails, a white tall collar, and a white crisp bowtie. He exuded the very essence of gentry as he stood in the foyer, softly tapping his white kid gloves against his black top hat.

"She should be down soon," he assured Daniel and Lily, who were seated on a finely-carved bench near the entryway. It seemed Thomas was becoming accustomed to Eliza's fashionably late arrivals.

From the hall just shy of the stairs, Eliza smiled. Just then, she descended the stairs, her elegant gown of white satin adorned with a pink chiffon overlay gathered in the back. The skirt flowed gracefully, adding to the allure as she moved down the staircase. Her creamy, white skin and Gibson-girl hairstyle seemed to radiate effortless beauty, though she had spent the majority of the afternoon preparing for the evening.

His gaze soft on her, Thomas remarked, "You are a vision of loveliness." With a gentle gesture, he took her hand and brought it to his lips. She wore no gloves, as her sleeves ended in a point on the back of her hand. She felt the warmth of his lips as he touched her.

"I believe I am being escorted by the most handsome man attending the ball tonight," she said, a perky little smile gracing her lips. She handed him her full-length, velvet, cream-colored cape lined with gray fur, and slipped her hands into the matching muff.

"You both rival the elegance of royalty," Lily sighed wistfully, greeting Eliza. Daniel rolled his eyes, but followed it with a smile.

"Thank you, Lily. You look lovely as well," Thomas replied, taking the lead to the waiting carriage.

Daniel interjected, kissing his wife lovingly on the cheek. "My sentiments exactly. You look beautiful, Lily."

As they traveled along in the coach, the foursome enjoyed sharing some of their favorite New Year's traditions. "Certain foods including roast pork, bread and salt, and Spotted Duck pudding are always served on New Year's Day in our house because they symbolize luck, progress, and abundance," Eliza said.

"Well, I think one of the most delightful traditions is kissing at midnight to bring good luck and happiness for the coming year," Lily grinned, looking at Daniel and batting her eyelashes.

Eliza was certain that a kiss would be part of the night's festivities for Lily. Daniel's love for his wife was apparent. Perhaps she would even receive a kiss. Although she and Thomas had shared a few kisses in the privacy of her home, would he be comfortable kissing her in a public setting?

"Writing New Year's resolutions for yourself or someone else is always so amusing," Daniel said. "Last year, the one I drew out of a hat read, 'I would like to stop snoring during church.'" Laughter burst out in the carriage.

"Well did you?" Thomas asked drolly.

Daniel chose to ignore the comment and pointed out that they had arrived at the Saunders family estate. The appearance of the estate was most impressive. Under the clear starlit night, lanterns glowed a soft yellow, set among potted evergreen plants adorned with shimmering ribbons.

As they entered, Admiral and Mrs. Saunders greeted them

warmly. Jane, standing nearby on the arm of Emmett, evoked femininity in the gold-embroidered, off-shoulder dress that accentuated her tiny waistline. Emmett reached out to shake hands with Thomas and Daniel. He smiled at Eliza, appearing as if nothing had occurred between them. Eliza maintained a cordial face, concealing the discomfort she was feeling.

Within the grand ballroom, a chandelier hung in the center of the ceiling. Garlands of evergreen cascading from the chandelier at its center, created a captivating display that extended gracefully throughout the expansive room. Several decorated Christmas trees were scattered about. A variety of foods enticed guests as they were artfully arranged on multiple tables.

As Thomas and Eliza entered the dance floor, they were handed poppers, which added to the festive mood. Loud popping sounds could be heard throughout the room. Guests with paper hats on them bobbed up and down as they danced and laughed.

Even though it was merely a superstition, Admiral Saunders insisted bells would be ringing at midnight to ward off evil spirits. He also wanted a coin placed in each person's pocket to usher in a prosperous new year. The most amusing part of the evening was where each guest wrote a New Year's resolution.

Emmett read from the first paper picked. "I must stop smoking in my sleep," drawing chuckles from the group.

Next was Jane, who read, "I must walk with my right foot on the left side." Her statement drew a ripple of laughter and curious glances from others. She looked charmingly at Emmett, who responded in kind. Their brief exchange hinted at a tentative connection between them.

"I would like to learn to ride a bicycle backward." Daniel's resolution brought a round of laughter from the guest. The amusement continued as each person took their turn reading, adding to the jovial spirit of the evening.

As the night progressed, and the laughter and chatter filled the room, Emmett, catching Eliza's eye, approached her with a serious, but friendly expression. "May I have a word with you, Miss Wentworth? If you would be so kind, it won't take long," he promised. Considering their last uncomfortable discussion in the coach, she wanted to keep some distance between them.

She paused, mulling over the situation and gave him a nod of approval. Reluctantly, Thomas relinquished her hand and asked Jane Saunders for the next dance.

Walking to the side of the room, Emmett began, "Miss Wentworth, I wish to apologize for my behavior at our last meeting. I wasn't considering your feelings, and was thinking only of myself. Unfortunately, my ego got in the way of my reasoning, and I am sorry for questioning the young man for coming to your aid. Your comments have given me much to think about."

Eliza thought for a moment before she replied. "I appreciate your forthrightness, Mr. Bentley. But there is another matter that bothers me."

"What is that, Miss Wentworth?" Emmett asked.

"The unkind remarks you made about Thomas, especially as we were his guests in his home, were not very gentleman-like," Eliza said frankly.

"I have thought about those as well, Miss Wentworth, and regret saying them. My only excuse lies in being an only child. I've harbored envy toward Thomas and Daniel, yearning for the camaraderie they share. The absence of a brother has left me wanting. Despite them including me in family gatherings, I've failed to appreciate it, and will remedy that going forward. Thomas is a man I admire and he deserves the best."

She considered Emmett's words before saying, "Thank you, Mr. Bentley. I appreciate you making this effort tonight."

"Am I forgiven?" He had not previously shown that sincerity, which appealed to Eliza.

Smiling, Eliza said, "Yes, of course. In my opinion, all the Bentley men are gentlemen."

Emmett bowed and smiled. "Thank you, Miss Wentworth."

As he walked away, Eliza reflected on their conversation, she felt a wave of relief and satisfaction. She joined Thomas, who had been watching with interest.

"Did things go well?" he asked.

"Yes," Eliza replied with a smile. "Emmett was very pleasant and even apologized for his past behavior. I told him all was forgiven and I'm glad we could be friends again."

Thomas took her hand and smiled pleasantly, "Now I'm aware of another of your many talents. "

"Oh, and what is that?" she teased.

"Peacemaker."

She blushed. "If you could accept your cousin's apology, so could I."

"Emmett speaks highly of Miss Saunders. With time, possibly something more may come of it," Thomas added.

"Perhaps, if he can settle down rather than flitting about like a butterfly does from flower to flower," Eliza said with skepticism.

"Point taken," he agreed. "I would like to show you a little spot I've found."

He guided her through the grand ballroom, leading her towards the far end where an arched entryway with embroidered drapes pulled back on either side. Inside was a charming alcove, its walls covered with lovely embossed gold wallpaper. A plush cranberry-colored settee was near a flickering fireplace and glowing sconces casting a warm light. Adding a touch of the Christmas season was a small table with poinsettias set on it.

Surveying the cozy nook, Eliza said, "You're always full of surprises. How ever, did you find this spot?"

"When I asked Admiral Saunders if there was a place in the ball-room for a private conversation, he pointed this out to me." Thomas gestured to the settee, and they both sat. Eliza leaned against him, her head gently resting on his shoulder.

"I never imagined your returning to Bentley Manor would result in such happiness. Each time we are together, I look forward to the next," she said.

Thomas lifted her hand to his lips and kissed it tenderly. "I feel the same way, Eliza. I don't want us to be apart. I love you, and want you by my side always."

"Thomas, what are you saying?" she asked, looking at him with a mix of surprise and anticipation.

He knelt down on one knee. "Dearest Eliza, will you do me the honor of becoming my wife?" She gasped as she felt a thrill go from her head to toes.

"Yes, Thomas. Yes." Tears of joy began forming.

Upon standing, he opened a small round velvet box and removed a large diamond set in white gold, reflecting light like tiny mirrors. "It's called a solitaire," he said, slipping the ring on her finger. "If you would prefer, it can be exchanged for a more traditional setting with a gemstone surrounded by small diamonds."

"I love it. It's perfect." Her eyes sparkled like two bright stars in the heavens.

Wrapped in each other's arms, they shared several kisses.

"I never expected a proposal tonight, Thomas," Eliza said, looking up, her face radiant with happiness.

"I had planned on proposing later tonight in the privacy of your home." He held her face in his hands, and kissed her again. "But I didn't want to wait any longer."

"It's almost midnight. I've been looking everywhere for you two," Daniel said, appearing through the opening way, a silly paper hat on his head ready to fall off. Seeing the romantic scene before him, his voice trailed off.

"We've just become engaged!" Thomas announced with unabashed pleasure. Eliza proudly displayed her ring.

"Congratulations. I couldn't be happier for both of you." Daniel shook both their hands.

Word of their engagement spread faster than a whirling dervish, twirling through the room. There were shouts of cheers and applause. Lily was thrilled, and hugged Eliza, welcoming her to the family.

"Splendid news," Admiral Saunders declared when he was told of Eliza and Thomas's engagement. Examining Eliza's ring closely, he said, "This is the finest solitaire I've seen. No doubt from one of the diamond mines in Africa." Thomas gave an affirmative nod. "Very lovely, Miss Wentworth."

"How perfect you became engaged at our New Year's Gala," gushed Mrs. Saunders, giving Eliza a hug. Despite their difference in age, the two had formed a genuine friendship. Emmett and Miss Saunders made their way over to the happy couple.

"Congratulations, Thomas!" Emmett said, shaking Thomas's hand. "Miss Wentworth, you have captured the heart of a remarkable man." Thomas looked surprised at his cousin's words, but Eliza was delighted. Clearly, Emmett was already working hard at turning over a new leaf.

At midnight, the room was filled with the joyful peal of bells, rung by two footmen stationed by the entrance. Laughter, good wishes, and kisses filled the room, while poppers and colorful streamers added to the festivities. Amidst the joyous chaos, Thomas kissed Eliza in a brief, but meaningful kiss. After she looked at him, her eyes reflected the joy she was feeling. He gently cupped her cheek, and they kissed again, this time with a tenderness that spoke of their love for each other.

It was well after midnight when he helped Eliza out of the coach.

"Please, don't dilly-dally. It is cold out here." Daniel shifted in his seat as Lily slept comfortably, her head resting on her husband's shoulder.

"I'll do my best!" Thomas called out half-heartedly, hurrying Eliza along and shielding her from the chilly wind. They huddled together until they entered the manor, closing out the cold.

In the dimly-lit entryway, Thomas removed Eliza's cloak and drew her into his arms. Their kiss began tenderly, a gentle brush of lips, but grew more passionate, conveying the love that bound them together and the excitement of their engagement. She felt as though the sparks between them could light up the room. As she touched his cheek, she felt the slight stubble of a beard beginning to form.

"I do love your dimpled chin," she said, tracing it with her finger.

"Good, because it's there to stay." He kissed her fingertips.

"Tonight seems like a dream. I hope I don't wake up tomorrow and find that it was," Eliza said.

"It's not a dream," Thomas replied firmly, gently caressing her cheek. "We have a promising new year ahead of us. How do you feel about a four-month engagement? I thought we could marry in April, and celebrate your birthday on our honeymoon." Their foreheads were touching. She saw several wet marks on his linen shirt, a result of her tears.

"That would be lovely." She sighed contentedly. "I think spring is a perfect time to have a wedding. It's such a nice time of year, so many lovely flowers."

"I am certain my parents will come. Travel is much better that time of year."

As the clock chimed one, Eliza fluttered her eyelashes playfully. "Remember, you mustn't dilly-dally."

"Never," he smiled.

Taking hold of his lapels, she reached up and kissed him. "I love you."

"And I love you, Eliza." The clock chimed quarter past the hour.

"Mother has arranged for hot bricks to be put in the coach's metal box."

"She thinks of everything, please thank her for me," Thomas said.

"Well," Eliza said, "almost everything. I'm quite sure she did not think I would become engaged tonight."

"If she spoke with your father, she most likely did. I talked with him earlier this week, and he gave his blessing."

"Thank you, Thomas. That means the world to me."

"I like to follow protocol—most of the time, that is." He winked and looked up at the kissing ball.

"I must take advantage while it is still hanging in the doorway."

"It won't be here much longer. My father insists that all Christmas decorations must be down by The Twelfth Night, January sixth. If not, he feels it will bring bad luck," Eliza explained.

"Do we really need mistletoe?" Thomas murmured with a smile, giving her a parting kiss. "Good night, my dearest Eliza, soon to be Lady Elizabeth Mae Bentley."

She watched from the doorway as Thomas headed to the coach. When he turned back to look at her once more, she blew him a kiss. A sleepy-eyed footman carrying a box trudged behind him. She wondered how she could be so blessed. Today was one of the happiest days of her life.

AN UNFORESEEN CALAMITY

*T*he next few weeks were rather dismal. All the festivities were over, and the skies remained overcast most of the time. However, there was a bright spot amidst the gloom—Eliza's pending marriage. It was hard for her to believe she had become engaged on New Year's Eve. She thought back at the time that she knew Thomas as reserved and always proper, now she had discovered the playful and charming side he shared with those he was closest to.

Eliza and Thomas chose Wednesday, April fourteenth, for their wedding day, a day of the week some believed symbolized balance and stability. With only two months to go, Eliza and her mother visited a stationery shop in town to have invitations prepared. They selected cream-colored parchment paper adorned with family crests, each invitation to be elegantly engraved. Those going to out-of-town guests were to be sent immediately to allow ample time to prepare for the journey. Soon after, written confirmation of attendance began to arrive.

Eliza was thrilled when her cousins Lauren and Courtney Johnson wrote they would be delighted to attend. Growing up, she had been close to her cousins, and cherished the memories of riding horses through the countryside and wading in a shallow stream with them.

A timeless, elegant silver tea service arrived from Grandmother Ruth Harris, accompanied by a heartfelt letter. Though she deeply wished to attend, her grandmother had recently been recovering from an illness and was still concerned about her health. Eliza loved the exquisite tea set that reminded her of the rich hot chocolate her grandmother often served while sharing stories of ancestors from bygone eras. It was a treasure Eliza would always value and use in her home.

Even Julia's mother sent her best wishes, along with a beautifully-bound edition of Alfred Lord Tennyson's poems. Laura, Julia's sister, and her husband, Neville Sinclair, also sent their regards and confirmed they would be attending the wedding.

As Eliza eagerly awaited the arrival of her wedding gown, which had been ordered from Paris, she prepared a special keepsake box, containing the traditional items that brides cherish. Among them were something old (a beaded purse from Grandmother Wentworth), something new (exquisite pearl earrings from Thomas), something borrowed (a lavender sachet from Daisy), and something blue (a garter trimmed in blue). The last item in her box was a sixpence to place in her shoe for good luck.

Margaret was to be her matron of honor, and Daniel would serve as Thomas's best man. When Pamela was asked to be the flower girl, she asked Eliza if flowers would be pinned all over her dress. Eliza had laughed and explained she would wear a white pinafore dress and would scatter petals from a glass bride's basket down the church aisle. Ned would follow behind in a dark blue velvet suit with knee pants, carrying a cushion bearing the wedding rings.

As Eliza went through all the wedding plans in her mind, she lingered on the thought of the wedding breakfast that was to be served at Wentworth Manor directly after the church ceremony. The details swirled in her mind. She found herself needing to clear her mind and get some fresh air.

The gray clouds cast a soft filter over the landscape, muting colors and creating a sense of tranquility. She skirted around puddles from yesterday's rainfall. Eliza's fashionable corduroy coat looked lovely, but it offered little protection against the chilling wind that caused her hair to sway and dance with its gusts. Despite the cold, she found it invigorating.

As she strolled along, noticing the clusters of yellow crocuses popping up among the patches of snow, she thought of the upcoming honeymoon, the location of which Thomas was keeping a secret. She tried to coax the destination from him, but to no avail. In anticipation, he had sent her a lovely dress in her favorite shade of blue to wear on their honeymoon, as was customary for the groom to do.

Returning from her walk, she saw a rider leaving the manor, and couldn't help but wonder about the delivery. Perhaps it was something related to her upcoming nuptials. Could it be her wedding dress? Seeing riders come and go had become quite common lately, signaling that a gift or something connected to the wedding had just been delivered.

Handing her coat to a footman and approaching her father's study, she heard her mother frantically speaking in a loud voice. "This is just terrible. I just don't understand how this could be happening to us!"

She was stunned when she entered the room to see her father's flushed face, his trembling hand clutching an official-looking paper. Her father, always the epitome of confidence and bravado, now looked frantic, revealing the weight of the upsetting news he had just received.

"I have very bad news," he began. "I've been accused of misusing company funds from the investment group I belong to, and there's a letter from the bank stating that the loan I took out using our estate as collateral, is due in a fortnight."

"Surely this is a misunderstanding. Some terrible injustice has been done," Eliza practically shouted, her voice trembling with shock and distress.

"Father, how could such a thing happen? This can't be true. You've alway upheld the highest standards and expected the same from others. What can be done to clear up these terrible accusations and to clear your name?" Her distress was evident and her face grew pale.

"I'm afraid not. It's all true," her father sadly admitted. "I've made some grave errors. I could go to prison for what I have done."

"This just can't be," Eliza said in disbelief. "Father, you would never do such a thing. There must be some mistake." He sat quietly, not uttering a word.

As harsh reality set in, a deep sadness enveloped her. Her father, her hero, now appeared as a silent figure amidst the whirlwind of chaos, swirling through her thoughts. She felt as if she were trapped in a horrible nightmare with no way to escape. As she stood there, her hurt turned to indignation. She wanted to offer compassion, but the weight of the situation overwhelmed her, and her initial reaction of denial turned into anger.

"Father, how could you?" She faced him with disbelief.

"I did it for you and your mother, Eliza." He attempted to justify his actions.

"Did you? Or was it to satisfy your own pride?" Frustrated, her voice trembled with anger.

"You interfered in a possible engagement when I was eighteen, and now you have destroyed my chance of happiness with Thomas. He will want nothing to do with me or our family." She stomped out of the room. The slamming of her bedchamber door echoed down the hall.

Eliza cried herself to sleep that night, and awakened early the next morning, puffy-eyed, yet determined. She sat at the desk in the sitting room, and slowly began writing a note to Thomas.

"My lord, this note just arrived from Wentworth Manor," Kingsley said, approaching Thomas with a small silver tray. He recognized it as being from Eliza. As he and Eliza had been exchanging love letters, Thomas opened the seal, anticipating another sweet letter from her.

My Dear Thomas, I beg you to come. I must see you on a very urgent matter. Eliza.

Thomas crumpled the note and shouted, "Kingsley, have my horse saddled. I shall leave immediately."

"Very good, sir."

Riding toward Wentworth Manor, Thomas spurred his horse to a gallop. What could have happened to require his immediate presence? As he approached the estate, his mind raced with various possibilities. Upon arrival, he was shown into the sitting room where Eliza paced the floor. She looked as pale as parchment, her eyes bleary from crying.

"Oh, Thomas." She ran into his arms, taking several bracing breaths. Then she pulled away, removed her engagement ring, and slipped it into his hand. Her whole body trembled, but his brave warrior soldiered on.

"Thomas, circumstances have arisen concerning my family that make it impossible for us to marry," she said, attempting to hide her despair. "I am so sorry. I must release you from any further obligation to me." A tear rolled down her cheek.

Thomas stood, grappling with what could have possibly brought on such an action. It felt like all the air had been sucked out of the room. The ticking of the grandfather clock was the only sound that broke the silence, echoing the weight of the moment.

Knowing that a broken engagement could harm both of their reputations, especially hers, he asked, "What has brought this on? Have you fallen out of love with me already?" he said, his voice filled with concern.

"No, it is nothing like that," Eliza replied, her voice steady with resolve. "I'm doing this because of my love for you."

More bewildered than before, he guided her to the settee. "Forgive me, Eliza, for making light of this. What has happened?" he asked, his eyes searching hers for answers.

"A terrible calamity has befallen our family involving my father," Eliza went on. "Yesterday he received a court summons charging him with the misuse of funds relating to an investment company he is involved with. Additionally, he has taken out a loan that is due in fourteen days. He used Wentworth Manor as collateral."

"Oh, my dear, Eliza." He held her close as she leaned heavily on his shoulder.

"Where is the bank that issued the loan?" Thomas asked.

"London. It's from the Bank of England. Knowing that he must pay on the note, Father took the investment funds in hopes to invest and make enough money to replace the money borrowed from the bank. It is just a matter of time until this all becomes public. Not only will my family be in financial ruin with no assets, but my father will likely go to prison. Thomas, I must release you from any further obligation to me."

Thomas shook his head. This news was even more disastrous than he had imagined. He could not fathom Mr. Wentworth putting his family in such a precarious position. "If the terms are not met, what will your family do?"

"My sister and her husband have told us if we ever needed to be with them, we could. I don't imagine they were thinking of it being permanent."

His heart broke with his next words, but he had to consider his children. "I am so sorry, Eliza, this situation puts me in an untenable position. I need time to think about the gravity of the matter." With that being said, he bowed and left the room.

SHE HAD LOST THOMAS. Her joy of her impending marriage was shattered along with her broken engagement. The thought of never having him in her life, never being in his arms again was almost more than she could bear. The loss of her comfortable lifestyle paled compared to her dashed hopes for the future as Thomas's wife.

Eliza had envisioned herself in a beautiful church wedding surrounded by loved ones. Replacing those thoughts were ones about her father's inevitable imprisonment and the loss of her childhood home. Everything around her had lost its vibrancy and color, and she sat stunned and pale.

But she did not allow herself to wallow for long. Slowly, she moved to the desk, determined to do what she could to help, and began making a list. First, cancel the wedding gown ordered from Paris. Second, sell cherished furs and jewels. Her dreary task brought a fresh bout of sobs.

Unexpectedly, Thomas burst into the room as the butler announced, "Lord Bentley."

Eliza looked at Thomas, his hair disheveled and perspiration on his forehead. His hat was missing. Closing the door, he helped her from the chair, gathering her into his arms. He looked into her eyes full of sorrow.

"Eliza, I refuse to abandon the one I love. How can I find happiness while you are suffering? I don't want to lose you, and I will do everything in my power to help your family."

"Oh, Thomas, are you certain? There is a great deal of money involved. It's asking too much. Your reputation and social standing could be destroyed, and you would be shunned right along with my family. I can't bear the thought of you and your children facing any scandal that would hurt them in any way."

"Hopefully, it will not come to that, Eliza," he said. "This is something that has to be worked through, and planned carefully, to know exactly what to do."

Reaching into his waistcoat pocket, he pulled out her engagement ring and said, "This needs to be back where it belongs." He slipped the ring back onto her finger, his touch reassuring and firm. Eliza reached up and pressed her lips to his.

"Thomas, you are the finest man I have ever known."

Overwhelmed by his willingness to sacrifice for her family, Eliza's heart swelled with gratitude. She recalled Emmett's comment about Thomas's refusal to help when he lost money on the horse races, contrasting it to Thomas's current display of selflessness. In fairness, her father should be left to pay for his bad deeds, just like Emmett had paid for his betting. But Thomas had now come to her rescue. She felt relief, joy, and shame.

"Now, if you would be so kind as to take me to see your father," Thomas said.

Eliza took Thomas by the hand and guided him to the study. She gently knocked on the door. "I need a moment to speak with him," she murmured.

On entering, she was shocked to see her father looking disheveled and very strained, almost like he was in a daze. Winston was stretched out near his master's feet, looking sad and reflecting his master's somber mood.

Eliza softly put her hand on his shoulder. "Father, I am very sorry about my outburst last night."

"What did you say that wasn't true? I have jeopardized your marriage and the future happiness of both you and your mother. Thinking of being separated from my family is unfathomable, but I have no one to blame but myself. My extravagance and blind faith in the false promises of the company I invested in has brought us to ruin. The Wentworth name will be held in disdain."

"There are hard times ahead, but I want to put things right between us," she said, kissing his cheek.

"Thank you, dear." He smiled weakly, putting his hand on hers. "Eliza, you are a fine daughter, and I love you." He always treated her with love, but rarely spoke of it.

"Thomas is outside, wanting to speak with you," she said. Her father waved Thomas in. Instinctively, Winston lifted his head and followed Eliza out of the room.

As she closed the door, she exchanged glances with Thomas and whispered, "Good luck. I love you."

"Lord Bentley, I assume you are here to withdraw your proposal to Eliza," Mr. Wentworth said regretfully.

Thomas shook his head. "I am here because of Eliza, not to break our engagement. Our wedding plans remain unaltered. Mr. Wentworth, I deeply regret this has happened, and I'm here to see if I can help. Eliza has explained the situation to me, and I suggest we make plans to leave for London immediately. I have connections there that may prove to our advantage."

Mr. Wentworth stared at Thomas, astonished. "I never expected you to offer such help," he said, his voice filled with disbelief.

"I want to help with this situation," Thomas replied earnestly. "I love your daughter deeply and care about your family. I don't want to distance myself from you. I'm here to offer my support in any way I can."

Mr. Wentworth's mind wandered back to the past. "I recall how quickly I removed Eliza from the young man she was associated with when his family fell on hard times. Now, I find myself in a similar situation and understand the gravity of it."

"Mr. Wentworth, I believe in second chances," Thomas said with empathy. "And hopefully we can secure one for you."

"I'm not sure I deserve that, Lord Bentley," Mr. Wentworth replied quietly. "But thank you."

The next two hours went by quickly as Thomas and Mr. Wentworth discussed possibilities. As Eliza and Thomas walked to the entryway door, Thomas said, "People only need to know that your father and I have left on business. Eliza, do not resign yourself to the inevitable abandonment of your home, or, worse yet, your father going to prison."

"I know you are strong," he continued. "Your help with the Suttons was remarkable, and I need you to be a warrior again. We are not dealing with the elements, but a situation just as perilous that will have a lasting effect on your family. Can I depend on you?"

"I will do my best. I'll be praying for you," she said, tears forming in her eyes.

After a brief kiss, he walked outside. "Your horse is ready, my lord," the groom said respectfully. Thomas mounted his horse and turned once more to see his sweetheart as she waved one of his handkerchiefs.

NAVIGATING THROUGH
DIFFICULT WATERS

The house was eerily quiet. As the lamps were lit and the draperies closed for the evening, in the sitting room, Mrs. Wentworth paced the floor, wringing her hands and dabbing her eyes. She was explaining to Margaret the possibility of losing the estate, and the unsettling threat that Mr. Wentworth could go to prison. Eliza, unable to sit still, stood at the side of the room, rocking Victoria in her pram. Her niece's sweet little face helped distract her from the distressing conversation going on.

Margaret sat, obviously trying to process this unbelievable disclosure. Finally she said, "Frederick and I have talked about the possibility of either of our parents needing to move in with us." She turned to her mother. "You and Father will always have a place to live, and of course, you too, Eliza, especially until things settle down."

"If this does settle down," Eliza huffed. Her frustration enveloped her like an invisible glass bubble she was trying to break out of but could not.

"Have you received any news from London?" Margaret asked.

"No. It's been almost a week since Father and Thomas left. They took paintings and other valuables with them, hoping to use them to pay off the loan at the bank. I tried to break off our engagement, but

Thomas insisted I go ahead with the wedding plans. The way things are now, I find that impossible," Eiza said gloomily.

Margaret pondered for a few minutes before speaking up. "What you need is a diversion."

"A diversion! Such as?" Eliza's expression reflected her doubt.

"Well, one thing you can do is decide on what household items you want to bring into your new home. I know there are some books you particularly love, and quilts made by our grandmothers."

"Going through jewelry, lingerie, and linens sounds so mundane with such pressing matters hanging over us." Eliza's eyes stung from unshed tears. "Besides, will there even be a wedding?" She knew at the moment she was not being a brave warrior. Uncertainty was robbing her of her courage.

Margaret tried once again. "Eliza, you've heard of a bridal shower?"

Eliza responded with a flat tone, "Of course, but they aren't held anymore."

"Actually, bridal showers are becoming popular again, especially in big cities," Margaret said. "My new neighbor, Janel Montague, who recently moved here from Canada, invited Lord Ainsley and me to dinner. Her husband mentioned that she's well-known for hosting delightful social gatherings. When she heard you were getting married, Eliza, she told me about a bridal shower she attended before leaving Ontario."

"What did Mrs. Montague say about it?" Eliza asked, showing a hint of curiosity.

"Well," Margaret replied, "she described that family and a few friends gather to honor the bride and bring small personal gifts or something for her new home. It's quite similar to a traditional after-noon tea, coming together for a pleasant social event. The quaint idea of showering gifts over the bride's head with an umbrella is no longer practiced. Instead, they place the gifts on a table. Mother and I could host one here. It would be the first in Amersham."

Eliza looked at her with disbelief. "How can you suggest such a thing? I can't possibly think of a bridal shower right now with Father and Thomas in London trying to sort out this financial mess."

"I'm sorry if this is upsetting you," Margaret said gently. "I didn't mean to be insensitive. We wouldn't hold it until things are settled in London. I don't want this to be awkward for any of us, but we can keep it in mind."

"I don't know," Mrs. Wentworth said. "I'm worried people will think we need charity?"

"I don't think so," Margaret replied reassuringly, "when they understand the purpose of the shower. But let's not concern ourselves with that right now. We can focus on other wedding preparations." Feeling the tension, she added, "I think I had better see to Victoria," and left the room with her daughter.

Margaret's words offered some comfort, yet Eliza remained restless. Picking up a book, her eyes scanned the pages, but her mind wandered. Conversation at dinner felt burdensome, so she excused herself early and went to her bedchamber. Lying in bed, her mind replayed the unsettling image of white umbrellas filled with pebbles pouring over her head. With a sudden jolt, she walked to the window. Through the open curtains, the shimmering moon in a lonely sky cast eerie shadows on the adjacent wall. In that quiet moment, she wondered if Thomas was gazing at the same night sky.

In London, moonlight spilled over the city, casting a small sliver of light on Thomas's desk. He and Mr. Wentworth were staying at the Savoy Hotel, rather than with his parents, to keep the matter private. With a heavy sigh, he set aside the private detective's report. The investigation revealed that the company Mr. Wentworth had invested in was a fraud. Posing as a railroad company offering high returns, it had lured Mr. Wentworth with promises of substantial profits in a short time. However, the report concluded that the company was a deceptive scheme designed to entrap investors. The perpetrators had vanished, with the last sighting of them boarding a ship leaving England.

The flickering lamp signaled the lateness of the hour. Moving to adjust the heavy drapery, Thomas glanced up at the moon. Thoughts of Eliza under the same lunar glow brought a measure of comfort to him. Closing the drapery and succumbing to fatigue, he extinguished the lamp.

The morning was gray and damp from a light rain as Thomas and Mr. Wentworth approached the formidable Bank of England on Threadneedle Street. It appeared like a fortress not to be trifled with. They were greeted by Mr. Joseph Miller, a distinguished banker, with the traditional pinstripe suit and black Locke loafers. On his desk was a placard with his name and title, Bank Vice President, alongside a row of meticulously organized leather-bound ledgers and a brass inkwell.

"Allow me to introduce Lord Bentley," Mr. Wentworth said. "He is my future son-in-law."

"It's a pleasure to meet you, Lord Bentley," Mr. Miller said as Lord Bentley extended his hand. Mr. Miller shook it firmly. "I handled some matters for your grandfather, Lord Harold Bentley, and I'm acquainted with Lady Bentley as well."

Thomas leaned forward slightly, his tone measured yet hopeful. "Perhaps at a future date, we could discuss some of my holdings that I'm considering transferring to this bank." He hoped the idea of future business might aid in the negotiations for Mr. Wentworth. "We're here to discuss the loan Mr. Wentworth borrowed from the bank. My understanding is that one-third of the Wentworth estate is entailed, and the note is due in two weeks."

"That is correct," Mr. Miller responded. "There are loans from the past that were paid off successfully. However, this most recent one is a short-term loan and has now come due. Is there a problem taking care of this?"

Thomas began, "Mr. Wentworth used the borrowed funds from the bank to invest in a company that has since proven fraudulent. I have a report here from a private investigator." He handed the report to Mr. Miller, who quickly skimmed through it.

Mr. Miller looked up and said slowly, "Mr. Wentworth I regret that this loan, taken out in good faith, has been lost to such a disreputable company. These thieves are among the worst I've encountered. They entice reputable businessmen to invest, by initially paying a quick sizable dividend. This creates a facade of credibility that draws in others. Once their coffers are full, they disappear."

Mr. Wentworth sat, dejected.

"We've brought a number of valuable items from the manor with more to come to be authenticated and valued," Thomas said. "It's our intention to use these to help pay off the loan. Any remaining amount will be covered by my railroad stocks. If you are agreeable, we will proceed with this plan."

"Because such a transaction will take longer than two weeks, I will need the approval of the bank president, who is due back tomorrow," Mr. Miller said, taking out a ledger and quill pen. "Where can I reach you?"

"We are staying at The Savoy Hotel. Thank you for your time, Mr. Miller. We look forward to hearing from you soon." Thomas and Mr. Wentworth took their leave.

The following day, Thomas and Mr. Wentworth visited the office of Brent Gilbert, Man-of-Law. Mr. Gilbert was a highly-regarded solicitor. He appeared to be nearing fifty and was impeccably dressed in a light gray suit. His complimentary ascot was perfectly tied, and he had unusually white teeth.

Mr. Gilbert greeted them and stated confidently, "I will contact the plaintiffs to see if they're willing to settle out of court and drop all charges against you, Mr. Wentworth. Investment companies often prefer to avoid any negative publicity, which works in your favor. If you're agreeable, I suggest negotiating to replace the funds plus five percent interest. Offering to surrender your shares in the company will give you additional leverage."

"What are our chances of them accepting this offer?" Mr. Wentworth asked.

"I believe they are good," Mr. Gilbert replied. "Avoiding court is more economical and keeps things private. However, if necessary, I'll prepare all the legal documents, and arrange for a barrister to present the case."

As they left Mr. Gilbert's office, Mr. Wentworth's shoulders sagged and he walked slowly, leaning on Thomas's arm. "It is impossible for me to meet the terms. Lord Bentley, the future looks dismal, and I am sorry that you have been brought into this."

"Please call me Thomas, and it was my choice to come with you, Mr. Wentworth," Thomas asserted. "We're not done for yet. We just have to keep moving forward and do the best we can. Hopefully, with divine assistance," he said gently, "we can navigate through this ordeal with a positive outcome."

"Thank you, Thomas," Mr. Wentworth said, looking like he was near collapsing. "And please, call me Henry."

Thomas hailed a hansom, calling out to the driver, "The Savoy."

Mr. Edwards passed by the dining room window at Wentworth Manor for the fourth time, accompanied by Alec, a stable hand experienced with the handling of firearms. They appeared to be inspecting the exterior of the house, focusing on the doors and windows.

"I don't understand why Mr. Edwards and his stable hand are here. They have been lurking around for days, and it makes me nervous." Mrs. Wentworth waved her fork in the air.

"Mother, the constable told Daniel that two homes, not far from here, have been burglarized, and said we need to take extra precautions, especially at night," Eliza explained for the third time.

"Our staff is fully capable. Is it not enough that we have to worry about your father, but now we have to worry about housebreakers?" It was no use trying to convince her mother.

Margaret added, "And then there is the presence of Daisy. I don't think Mr. Edwards minds being here at all."

"Nothing escapes you, Margaret." Eliza smiled, shaking her head.

Eliza spent the evening trying to read a book, but her thoughts kept wandering, and she finally gave up and went to bed. Experiencing another restless night of tossing and turning, Eliza got up and went to the window, drawn to the moonlight cutting through the darkness. Its light revealed eerie shadows of spindly branches resembling skeletal fingers reaching out to grasp something. Suddenly, she saw the outline of two men rounding the side of the house. She knew immediately it was not Mr. Edwards or Alec, or any of their staff.

Quickly, she lit a candle and slipped a wrapper over her nightgown. Creeping down the staircase, she looked around for help, but no one was in sight. The only noise was Winston's barking, coming from the dining room. Through the lace curtains on the French doors, she saw the silhouettes of two men moving towards the entrance. Her heart beat faster as she gasped with terror.

A pane of glass shattered as the doorknob began twisting. Suddenly two men were illuminated, a shotgun pointing at Eliza.

Her shriek echoed throughout the manor and her world spun. Then, Eliza fainted.

JUBILATION OR LAMENTATION

$\mathcal{I}$nside the manor, the butler announced Daniel's arrival.

When Mrs. Wentworth saw him, she exclaimed, "Mr. Bentley, how can we ever thank you?" Mrs. Wentworth came forward, extending her hand toward him.

"I'm grateful your family is safe," Daniel replied. "Tell me what happened, Mrs. Wentworth. I just saw Constable Evans taking the house-breakers away."

"Eliza can tell you. She's the one that saw them," Mrs. Wentworth said.

"Last night I couldn't sleep, so I went to the window and stood looking out," Eliza began. "I often do that when I'm restless. When I saw two men lurking outside next to the house, I acted impulsively and rushed down looking for help. But no one was around except Winston, barking furiously at the French doors in the dining room."

"Eliza, if they had succeeded in breaking in, what were you planning to do? You could have been injured or worse. The thought just makes me shudder," Margaret interjected.

"Where were the footmen?" Daniel asked.

"Unfortunately, the footmen," Mrs. Wentworth said, "who were supposed to be on duty were not. They admitted they took the warning lightly and were off playing cards. They've been repri-manded and will lose their evening privileges for the next week. Such a breach of trust will not be tolerated again. Go on, Eliza, dear."

"It was dark, so I could only see their shadows. But one of them broke a pane of glass, and his hand reached in to find the doorknob. I was terrified. Suddenly a light shone on them, and I saw someone pointing a shotgun at them. Everything seems a little blurry after that," Eliza put her hand on her head, remembering the fear that had engulfed her.

"Yes," Mrs. Wentworth added, "Eliza was in a daze for a bit. Later, Mr. Edwards told us he and Alec had spotted the intruders with binoculars. They hurried to the house with some sort of lantern."

"I gave them a dark lantern, like the ones the police use," Daniel explained. "It's called that because it remains dark until you open the shutter that shields the light."

Mrs. Wentworth sighed with relief. "I'm so glad you sent those men over. I never really expected anything like this to happen," she admitted.

The tension they had all been feeling began to subside as they sat together, sharing tea and scones. No one had eaten breakfast that morning, but with the immediate danger over, the warm food was comforting.

Satisfied that the ladies were recovering from the ordeal, Daniel took his leave from Bentley Manor. Not long after his departure, a footman appeared at the door carrying a note on a silver tray.

"This just arrived from London," he announced.

Eliza quickly picked up the envelope, recognizing Thomas's writing.

"It's from Thomas," she said eagerly as she opened the letter. "He writes they are working on negotiations and plan to return in a matter of days. He also hopes that we are all well," Eliza said. "I can't wait to see them. This waiting is so frustrating. My thoughts run rampant from thinking things will be fine to Father being put in jail."

"Dear, you are doing very well, especially given the circumstances. You've been able to help plan the wedding breakfast, and have had the gown you wore on New Year's Eve altered for the wedding," Mrs. Wentworth assured her daughter. Margaret came alongside and put her arm through Eliza's.

"I am trying to remain positive, but it is exhausting. I was very excited to be wearing a white gown like Queen Victoria did when she married Prince Albert. Now I just look at the altered dress hanging in my room, and wonder what my wedding day will be like."

"I know the Queen has been an inspiration for you, Eliza. I brought something you might like. I think this is the right time to give it to you." A few minutes later Margaret returned with a book in her hand. "This is a copy of one of the Queen's journals. She has written over one hundred."

"This is just perfect. Thank you, Margaret," Eliza said, hugging her sister. The two felt uplifted, sharing their burdens. "Sometimes we forget that everyone faces challenges. The Queen's journals, along with her celebrations and duties, reveal the difficulties she has faced with her children and personal struggles."

As the next week progressed, each day felt like an hour or two had been added to it. Eliza's worries gnawed at her like water corrodes a rusty pipe.

"I'm at my wit's end," Eliza said, flopping down ungraciously in a chair near her sister. "I've taken Victoria on walks, embroidered handkerchiefs for Thomas, and designed cards for you and the staff for Valentine's Day, which has now come and gone. We're nearly at the end of the month."

"February is the shortest month of the year," Margaret reminded her, clearly endeavoring to lighten the mood. Eliza was not amused and gave her sister an exasperated look.

"How can I continue to concentrate on my wedding with the uncertainty of what's happening?" Eliza wondered aloud. "Thomas insists he wants to marry me, but when this all becomes public, I don't want him to be subjected to censure. At least he'll be spared that. He will want to protect his children, and our engagement will be over." She pulled the curtain aside, revealing the overcast sky that seemed to reflect the dismal state of affairs in the room.

"I know Thomas is doing everything he can. I just don't know if it will be enough," Eliza sighed, her frustration evident in her voice. The only sound in the room was the crackling of the fire.

"Eliza, I know it's difficult," Margaret sympathized. "The longer we wait, the more challenging it becomes. Surely they must be on their way home by now."

The two sisters sat in subdued silence, having depleted their words of comfort for each other. The silence was broken by the forceful opening of the front door.

"They're here!" Eliza cried, rushing out into the hallway to greet her father and Thomas. She noticed their clothes were somewhat crumpled, and both looked like they needed a good night's rest. Thomas had the shadow of a beard.

"Eliza, please gather the family in the study," her father said wearily. She couldn't tell from his tone or Thomas's expression whether she was about to be elated or crushed. As they sat in the study, Eliza was eager but apprehensive to know the outcome of their journey.

Mrs. Wentworth complained that she was beginning to feel light-headed. Realizing her mother's breathing was rapid from taking in too much air, Eliza began gently rubbing her back. "Mother, breathe slowly through your lips as if you are whistling," Eliza instructed. Her father quickly moved to his wife's side, taking her hand. Soon her mother's breathing returned to normal.

"As you know," Thomas began, "we had two matters to settle—the use of unauthorized funds and clearing a loan issued by the bank. Unfortunately, the company the funds were invested in proved to be fraudulent."

"Can any of the money be reclaimed?" Margaret asked.

"It is highly unlikely. We hired a private investigator who traced the culprits boarding a ship." The family braced themselves for what was to come.

"We were fortunate in satisfying the investment partners by meeting their terms. It was settled out of court. There will be no further legal action. Additionally, a confidentiality agreement was signed, ensuring that this matter will not be discussed further with anyone," Thomas continued.

"There is no chance Father will have to go to prison?" Eliza asked.

"That's right, none," Thomas said with certainty. There was an audible sigh of relief in the room. "As for the loan from the bank, it is in the process of being paid off. The items we took to London and several others that will be sent as well, are being appraised to help clear the debt. The grandfather clock and other cherished possessions will remain here in the manor."

"Thomas has pledged his railroad stocks that are needed to pay off the loan," Mr. Wentworth interjected. "We were afraid the bank president would not agree to this, but after hearing Thomas's compelling case, he accepted the offer. The Wentworth Estate is no longer in jeopardy, and now Thomas has been added to the deed. He is the estate's trustee."

"What exactly does that mean?" Mrs. Wentworth asked, appearing to be somewhat confused.

"Mrs. Wentworth, as trustee," Thomas said kindly, "I will oversee all proceedings and profits, and the managing of the estate. Mr. Harrison, my steward, will help until one can be hired. The manor will continue on just as it is now in the Wentworth name. This is your home and will remain as such. You will have a say in any changes that are made."

"At a later time," he added, "I want to discuss with you a plan for developing the property so it is self-sustaining and eventually generating revenue. To accomplish such an enterprise requires capital, which provides a logical explanation for the present liquidating of much of the estate's furnishings."

It took the family several minutes to process this information, but all the results had proved positive and their fears dissolved. Their sense of relief was almost tangible, being replaced by a rejuvenation of energy.

Mrs. Wentworth clasped her hands and broke into tears, first hugging her husband and then Thomas. "We're forever grateful, Lord Bentley."

"Please call me Thomas."

"Thank you, Thomas, and please call me Marjory," Mrs. Wentworth said, smiling for the first time in days.

"Lord Bentley, with your permission, I would also call you by your Christian name," Margaret said, clasping both his hands in hers.

"Of course."

"Thomas, you have my deepest gratitude. You have done a great service for our family." Margaret wiped away her own tears.

Mr. Wentworth cleared his throat, obviously choking up while trying to express his thoughts. "I shall never forget your help and kindness." He could manage to say no more.

"Well, I think it is time for me to take my leave, so you can have your time together," Thomas said as he started walking down the hallway. As he turned to leave, Eliza ran into his arms, and cried silently on his shoulder. Softly stroking her hair, he whispered comforting words.

"Thomas, there were many times these past days that I have been discouraged, consumed with worry," she admitted. "I kept waiting, hoping, and praying."

"I understand. I was weighed down with the daunting task looming ahead. Knowing that you had faith in me and that we were both praying for help, gave me the courage to continue on. It was nothing short of a miracle that the bank accepted our offer."

"But what of your stocks? You have put so much time and thought into your future investments," Eliza objected.

"I am grateful I could use them. I still have some remaining shares in the railroad company I have invested in. It looks promising that trains will travel between Amersham and London in a year or two."

"But you sacrificed the money you set aside for a residence in London. When you return there, you do not want to live with your parents again," she murmured, her voice tinged with hesitation.

"My dearest Eliza," Thomas replied tenderly, lifting her chin, and gazing into her beautiful sparkling blue eyes. "It is not a sacrifice when it is for a greater purpose. Our marriage means more to me than any wealth or investments, and my only thought was the well-being of you and your family. Perhaps because that was our goal, things worked out as they did."

"Thomas, you are truly remarkable. I love you," she said, giving him a radiant smile.

"I love you, my dear, Eliza. It's been a long, arduous two weeks for both of us." Recognizing the great obstacle that had been hanging over them, threatening their future happiness, they found solace in each other's arms. Thomas then gave her a lingering kiss.

"On our way here, we stopped briefly at Bentley Manor," Thomas said, his expression becoming serious. "Daniel told me of the attempted robbery. When I think of what could have happened to you...."

"But it didn't," she reassured him, gently placing her fingers on his lips. "Thank goodness for Daniel and his foresight in sending Mr. Edwards and Alec to watch over the manor."

Stepping outside, they felt drops of rain falling from a sky of white velvet, bringing refreshment to everything they touched. Leaning in and pressing his damp forehead against hers, they dispelled the uncertainty that had been weighing on them, forging a strong emotional bond.

JOURNEY TO THE CHURCH

Thomas and Eliza slipped away from the group gathered in the dining room, where Mrs. Wentworth was hosting a dinner party for the Wentworth and Bentley families. As they passed through the new sturdy oak doors that replaced the French doors, Eliza shivered slightly as the cool breeze penetrated her lightweight chiffon shawl. Sitting side-by-side on a bench beneath a cherry tree, its delicate pink and white blossoms perfuming the air, Thomas wrapped his waistcoat around her shoulders, holding her close. With her head resting on his shoulder, she was lost in the simple joy of his company.

"So this is a wishing tree," Thomas remarked, looking at the ribbons and notes attached to the branches amongst the pink blossoms of the cherry tree. "It amazes me, the interesting traditions that you ladies come up with."

"Isn't it delightful?" Eliza's eyes sparkled as she spoke. "Margaret asked all those attending my bridal shower to write a note of well-wishes that are now tied on the tree. Daisy's Irish Blessing is on there somewhere. She says it's an old Irish tradition, and wanted me to have one for good luck. Your parents added a wish today."

"How did you like my parents' wedding gift?" Thomas asked.

"It's a treasure," Eliza replied. "One we can keep in the family for years. It is such a lovely wedding chest. Your mother said it's made of walnut and created by John Woodland, an expert woodworker and friend of your family. The hand-carving, with our initials and date of our marriage on the front, is so unique. I am looking forward to filling it with linens and blankets."

"So, what do you think about our trip to Brighton?" Thomas asked nonchalantly, a playful smile on his face.

"Brighton! Is that where we're going on our honeymoon?" She sat up abruptly and threw her arms around him. "I went there several years ago, and have always wanted to go back. The sea breezes and charming streets are delightful. And best of all, I will be there with you. But why did you wait this long before telling me?"

"I know how excited you get, and how anticipation can make time seem longer," Thomas admitted. "So, I went ahead and made the arrangements. From London, we will travel on the South Coast Railway to Brighton. While in London, I thought we could visit your Aunt Elizabeth, as well as have a wedding photo taken. Most likely, you will want to buy a swimming costume."

"How exciting. I remember seeing a swimming costume in one of my ladies' magazines."

"Of course you did," he chuckled.

"It had a stylish top with a sailor collar, matching pantaloons, stockings, and shoes," Eliza described, her hand gesturing to her head. "The hat even had this cute nautical touch."

"You will look absolutely charming."

Eliza snuggled a little closer to him. "I always feel so safe and cared for when I am with you."

"I try," Thomas replied with a contented smile, "and I plan on doing that the rest of our lives."

"I will do the same for you and Ned and Pamela. Speaking of children...." She hesitated.

"Yes," he replied slowly, his voice measured and an eyebrow raised.

"I was wondering about the sleeping arrangements."

"Sleeping arrangements!" His voice went up an octave, and he almost slipped off the bench.

"Yes, the sleeping arrangements—that is, for the children."

"Oh!" Thomas visibly relaxed and resumed his upright position.

"What did you have in mind?" he asked, leaning forward with a hand on one knee.

"I've become aware that many parents are moving their children from the third floor nursery into rooms near their parents. That way they are close to their children and can more easily care for them, particularly at nighttime when they can spend time with them. Nursemaids and nannies can attend to the children's needs during the day, and keep the children in the nursery when parents are away."

"This is new to me," Thomas admitted.

"If you agree, two of the second-floor bedchambers could be redecorated for Ned and Pamela. They could even pick out their favorite colors and choose their own wallpaper."

"I'll take it under advisement." Thomas tapped his finger against his chin.

"Does that mean you will seriously consider it?" She pressed him further.

"I will take it under advisement. I like to research things before I make decisions, but I love that you're already concerned about the children's well-being. You will be a wonderful wife and mother." He leaned over and kissed her tenderly.

As they pulled apart, Eliza smiled, her expression turning thoughtful. "Until recently, I had never recorded an expenditure in my life," she said, thinking about the new responsibilities ahead. "Now I am beginning to understand costs. Mother and I have been meticulous in planning the wedding breakfast, and it will be very nice, but not extravagant. I have always dreamed of a traditional wedding, and that's what we are having. Thanks to Grandmother Wentworth's generous gift, we're using some of the funds for the breakfast and two cakes—a lovely white cake decorated with orange blossoms, and a groom's cake."

. . .

"ELIZA, dear, I am proud of you. You have learned from your family's problems rather than becoming bitter," he said.

"I worry about being the new mistress of Bentley Manor."

"There is no need to worry. As the new mistress, you will oversee the day-to-day operations along with Kingsley and Mrs. Adams. They are accustomed to making purchases, taking care of repairs, menus and the like. Before long, you'll become familiar with the workings of the manor. Your tenacity will be a great asset." She felt comfortable with that.

"The main thing is that I want you to have plenty of time for me, and of course, for Ned and Pamela." He reached over and intertwined their fingers.

"I can promise you that," she said, kissing him on the cheek.

"ELIZA, WAKE UP," her mother said, shaking her. "You will be late for your own wedding!"

Her eyes flew open. "Oh, no! I was so excited, I had a hard time falling asleep last night." Looking at the clock in her room, she realized that today's preparation had to be shortened considerably. The gown she had worn on New Year's Eve had been completely transformed and was now adorned with delicate lace draped across the front and gathered elegantly at the back.

Daisy helped her to get ready more quickly than Eliza would have liked, but it was her own fault. She was still quite pleased with the results, however.

"Lily once told Lord Bentley and I that we looked like royalty. Today I feel like a princess," she said, after viewing herself in the mirror.

"Oh, Miss Eliza, ye look like a vision straight out o' a fairy tale! Ye're the most beautiful bride I've ever laid eyes on. Lord Bentley is one lucky gentleman, he is!" Daisy declared as she placed the delicate full-length veil trimmed with orange blossoms on Eliza's head.

"Thank you, Daisy. You are such a dear. I don't know what I would do without you." She hugged Daisy.

Eliza joined her father by the entryway doors. He looked dapper in his midnight black suit and burgundy tie.

"Eliza, you look beautiful," he said. "I am honored to be your escort."

"You look well yourself, Father," she replied as he led her through the door. In the place of the usual coach stood a Landau carriage pulled by stately horses. Its ornate carvings and decorative molding, as well as the velvet seats, were very regal. Inside were garlands of roses, baby's breath, and ferns. The coachman and footman were dressed in elaborately-designed uniforms. Eliza, indeed, felt more like she was in a fairy tale than experiencing real life.

"This arrived this morning," Mr. Wentworth said, pointing to the carriage, "courtesy of Thomas."

"I mentioned to him I wanted a traditional wedding, never imagining such luxury," she said as a footman helped them into the carriage.

After traveling several miles, Mr. Wentworth said, "Eliza, aren't you even going to speak to me on your wedding day?"

"Of course. What would you like to talk about?" She was determined to stay calm and happy.

"I know you are upset with me for the pain I have inflicted on you and the family and the sacrifices Thomas has made. I had hoped for your forgiveness so we could be close again."

"I'm not harboring resentment about your actions that have been resolved," she said, much to his relief.

"Then what is it?" he asked in all sincerity.

She thought for a few moments. "It's hard to explain, Father. One day you are happy, and the next despondent. You speak as if you're a victim of what has happened, and act resentful that you have had to be helped."

Suddenly, the carriage came to an abrupt stop. Ahead was a flock of sheep sauntering across the road, slower than the lazy brook near

Eliza's home. The coachman, soon joined by the footman, acknowledged the delay.

"We'll yank up the canopy, Miss, so you won't catch too much of that sun and stay comfy. It shan't be too long before we get goin' again," said the coachman.

"Thank you," Eliza said.

She continued after the coachman and footman were otherwise occupied. "I have difficulty understanding why you shy away from the very man who helped us. He has never complained or spoken to me about this."

After a few moments, Mr. Wentworth spoke. "I am ashamed to say that you are right, Eliza. I have struggled with self-condemnation for my unwise actions, as well as my stubborn pride in having to be rescued. At times, embarrassment and self-reproach get the best of me. I'm having a hard time forgiving myself," Mr. Wentworth confessed.

Touched by his words and having a deeper understanding of how her father truly felt, she sighed and rested her head on his shoulder.

"I realize I am not the victim. My problems are a result of my decisions and actions. If it weren't for Thomas, I wouldn't be sitting here next to you, which indeed would be tragic."

"I hope you can start looking to the future, Father, and by doing so, the past will be less painful. I just want you to be happy, and know I love you."

"Eliza," her father said in earnest, "mending the relationship between Thomas and me will take some time, but I will make it happen. Before you leave on your honeymoon, I'll find an opportunity to speak with him. I want him to know how much I admire and appreciate him. He's like a son to me."

"I know that will mean so much to him, as well as to me," Eliza said softly.

"I have been thinking that I would like to be a part of the development of the Wentworth land for the plans going forward, and help wherever I can," Mr. Wentworth said. "I need to keep busy and not spend so much time dwelling on myself."

With their relationship restored, Eliza and her father could move forward. As did the coach, now that the sheep had cleared.

She opened her small jeweled bag, removed a dainty lace handkerchief, and handed it to her father. "Please take this to remember this day, and how much I love you."

He gave her a tender kiss on her forehead, reminiscent of how he kissed her as a child, putting the handkerchief in his vest pocket. As they approached the church, the sound of bells filled the air. They both felt the peace that comes from understanding one another.

Entering the chapel, her father whispered, "Your groom awaits you."

As she walked down the aisle on the arm of her father, smiles of family and friends greeted her from the flower-adorned pews. Her smile reflected the happiness she was feeling. As her father placed her hand in Thomas's, it was done with love and respect, a gesture of transferring responsibility.

Thomas, dressed in a navy suit, pristine white shirt, and black bowtie, was more handsome than ever. He exuded an air of distinction, but it was the kindness in his eyes and warmth of his smile that truly captivated Eliza.

As they gazed at each other, during the marriage ceremony, they prepared to embark on a new chapter of their lives together.

EPILOGUE—THREE YEARS LATER

*P*amela scampered down the hall in pursuit of her mischievous two-year-old twin brothers, Landon and Logan, making quite a ruckus as they moved along. Their nanny was not far behind, trying to keep up with them.

"Here comes double trouble," Daniel said to Thomas.

"Just wait until Hannah turns two," Thomas mused, gazing down at his niece, snugly cuddled in a lace-trimmed blanket in her pram. Her face lit up with a smile, revealing two little dimples.

"This little cherub!" Daniel looked affectionately at Hannah. "Really, Thomas," he said with all the gusto of a proud father.

The occasion they were celebrating today was the twins' birthday. Thomas's parents had traveled from London to Amersham by steam train. They found it pleasurable to travel in a comfortable passenger car for two hours. Emmett, now married to Jane Saunders, and their baby, Audrey, had also traveled from out of town. Emmett had found fulfillment in his marriage and declared Audrey was a beautiful child and looked just like her mother.

"I wonder what's keeping Eliza." Thomas pulled out the silver pocket watch Mr. Wentworth had given him. Going to the master bedroom and opening the door, the scent of gardenia filled the air.

Thomas saw Eliza dressed in a gown of softest gold at her dressing table, staring at the mirror.

"You look radiant, darling," Thomas said, leaning down and brushing a kiss lightly on her cheek.

"I don't feel radiant. I only feel queasy," she replied, pausing to exchange a playful glance at him.

Seeing the uneaten food on a nearby tray, he said, "Are our suspicions correct?"

She beamed. "Yes, we are expecting a child. I will soon be wearing my empire-waist dresses and adjustable corsets."

"That's wonderful," he said, taking her into his arms. "And to think we are having another baby. I hope *she* looks just like you."

"Or if a boy, *he* looks like you," she declared. "I have several names of boys that I have thought of."

"I like to see the baby first and determine if the baby looks like the name would fit," Thomas said.

"I'm excited to be having another child," she replied, absentmindedly adjusting her hair.

"Motherhood suits you. You have a radiance about you when you are having a new little one," he said, wrapping one of her curls around his finger.

"By the way, do you like my hair this way?" Her beautiful chestnut-colored hair was in loose flowing curls with a few flowers woven in.

"I do. I like it very much. Kate appears to be doing a fine job as your lady's maid," Thomas observed.

"Thank goodness Daisy had her sister take her place before she married Mr. Edwards. With a new little one on the way, I'll need Kate more than ever," Eliza said.

"Do you have any idea when that will be?" Thomas asked.

"Most likely the middle of November. We'll know more after I see Dr. Dyer," she said.

Moving to the window, Thomas saw Landon and Logan in the process of knocking down the bowling pins, a game set up for the older children. He watched as the two quickly moved to the refreshment table where Mrs. Wentworth, now Grandmother Wentworth, rescued the tablecloth that was about to be pulled off. Thomas grinned and thought it was time they join the others before everything was in disarray.

"Maybe our new addition will be a sweet, refined little girl," Thomas mused, his arm around Eliza, her skirt swishing gently as they strolled toward the garden.

"Perhaps, Thomas, but for now we should hurry along," she said, quickening her pace. He responded by giving her a lingering kiss.

"My dear," Thomas said with mock authority, "as hosts of the party, we can be fashionably late."

Printed in the USA
CPSIA information can be obtained
at www.ICGtesting.com
JSHW010807101224
74801JS00010B/20